MURDER BY PROXY

By the same author:

Whisper Murder, The Book Guild, 2002

Famous Brand Names, Emblems and Trademarks

MURDER BY PROXY

Marjorie Stiling

Book Guild Publishing

Sussex, England

First published in Great Britain in 2007 by
The Book Guild Ltd
Pavilion View
19 New Road
Brighton, BN1 1UF

Typesetting in Baskerville by
SetSystems Ltd, Saffron Walden, Essex

Printed in Great Britain by
CPI Bath

A catalogue record for this book is
available from the British Library

ISBN 978 1 84624 124 6

Chapter 1

He's up to something. The thought flashed through Helena's mind. It was as if she could smell something but couldn't place it. Or was it her imagination? But she had been married to Laurence long enough to know, when he voiced plans, his mind was already made up. And now, this latest plan was outrageous.

His silky voice was toned to prevent any possible opposition. 'Incidentally, Helena, I've just remembered . . .'

She looked up. She had been arranging hothouse flowers on the table in the wide front hallway. Laurence, still in his dark business suit, spoke from the open door of the library where he usually retreated with a cigar and listened to the six o'clock news.

'Yes, I've just remembered,' Laurence said: 'The Neville I've invited to dinner is a vegetarian.'

Oblivious to her sigh that such last-minute information meant adjusting the menu, Laurence crooned on in his smooth solicitor voice as though in his office, and she was a client. 'And about Canada, Helena, have you given it some more thought?'

She frowned but repressed any retort, there wasn't time. Why resume last night's serious topic of conversation when she had the table and the wines to check? And now that she had to see Julie, who was cooking the meal, to explain that one guest was a vegetarian and had to be catered for?

'As I said last night, Helena,' Laurence went on, 'buried here in a one-horse town – you don't want that.' He retreated into the library and closed the door.

She knew those were final words. His mind was made up, the matter closed. His plans were for them to leave here, their beautiful home in England's glorious West Country, to live in Canada. Plans she had heard last night for the first time. Plans which surprised her, and plans she didn't much like the sound of. They would need a lot of thinking about and a great deal of discussion and questions answered. Why, why, why? She feared they were plans that did not include Annaliese.

Helena recalled her mother's last words: 'Take care of Annaliese.' But Helena had needed no such request, already prepared to provide a comfortable home for her less fortunate twin sister – for love, not duty.

'Of course. Always,' she had promised, at the same time aware it would probably take a while for Annaliese to settle in with her and Laurence at The Firs. Helena thought they had managed the transition well. Admittedly this first year had been full of ups and downs, adjustments and compromises – mostly on her part – to make life run smoothly. She had ensured Annaliese was always kept happy with a supply of oil paints, boards and brushes; plenty of pencils and paper to sketch and to play Noughts and Crosses with Ben, Julie's little boy. And sensing that Annaliese's very presence and minor disabilities got on Laurence's nerves she had, as much as possible, kept Annaliese out of his way.

She finished arranging the hall flowers, and glanced at the closed library door. She seldom went in there. Books lined only two walls. A snooker table filled one end. The rest of the room with its high ceiling and Adam-style fireplace was taken up with leather armchairs and small oak tables within whisky reach, and large ashtrays. It was Laurence's den, and she was happy to leave him to it. These past

2

months she had reluctantly accepted that the charming man she had married four years ago had undergone a metamorphosis in both character and physique. But if she believed hearsay, he still had plenty of charm to spread elsewhere. She preferred not to listen to gossip. She could stand up for herself. Nevertheless in any domestic situation when some sort of confrontation was called for she chose her words carefully to avoid creating a bad atmosphere to which Annaliese would be sensitive. She aimed to give Laurence no cause for unkind looks towards Annaliese that she might see, or for him to say things which would hurt her if she could hear them; like his favourite invective to close any argument: 'What other man would put up with having his sister-in-law to live, especially one like her?'

She thought, if only he had asked last night, 'Helena, how would you like to live in Canada?' or 'What do you think of my idea, Helena?' He was once so charming. But accepting the way he had changed, and how his mind worked of late, she told herself that if he had consulted her at all, he was more likely to have said: 'How would you like to uproot, Helena? Go to Canada? Be free. Leave your sister. Put her in a Home. She can't speak properly. And she drags her foot.'

With the flowers finished, Helena calmed herself before going into the kitchen. She wouldn't let Julie see there was anything wrong; marital differences were embarrassing. She wondered if Julie had brought her little boy with her again this evening, or if she had managed to get a sitter. It seemed everyone had problems, and Julie's problem often made her testy.

The kitchen was Rayburn warm. Little spitting sounds came from within the oven, and a delicious smell of roasting meat. But she guessed it should not be difficult from the well-stocked cupboards for Julie to rustle up an alternative menu for Neville.

Julie was busy chopping something on a board, her willowy figure different from the usual image of a homely Aunt Bessie. When Helena told her what she wanted, Julie put her knife down on the scrubbed wooden table with what sounded like a little rap of irritation. 'It's a bit late, Mrs Bray. Wish you'd told me before.'

'Yes, I'm sorry, Julie. But I've only just found out.'

Julie wiped her thin hands on her flowered overall, considering. 'P'raps the vegetarian gentleman could just leave out the sirloin.' She paused for agreement, and when it didn't come, she begrudgingly said, 'I suppose I could do more carrots and calabrese.' She made it sound like a major task: 'And . . . well, this evening there is asparagus. I could do extra. But it all takes time. I'll have to adjust the butter . . .'

Helena was hoping Julie might bend to a vegetarian antipasto or tortellini, but she wouldn't push her. That was the worst of inheriting staff, it was as if they were doing you a favour. Julie had cooked for Laurence and his first wife. Being a single mother she had come back part-time, mostly evenings, just to oblige Laurence, so she said, when he had married Helena.

Going into the dining room, Helena cast an eye over the five settings. She moved a spoon here, a knife there. The carnations, straight from the glasshouse, reflected their red and gold in the highly polished mahogany table. Even though there would be three men, she had set a place for Annaliese next to her own. It would be easier to see that Annaliese had everything, and spare her having to ask for anything in her hollow, laboured sounds. They were perfectly understandable, but Laurence was apt to show his impatience, even in company.

From the large sideboard Helena selected several bottles of wine: a full red Rioja, some Bergerac 1988, and a lighter Chianti. She removed the corks, put the bottles on the table, and gave everything a last glance. Things had to be right. She should have realised when *she* was Laurence's secretary and, infatuated, had accepted her *then* charming employer's proposal of marriage, that Laurence's importance was very important to him.

The dining room door was open. But she felt rather than saw him pass by to go upstairs. The old floorboards were shrinking with the amount of heat needed to keep the lofty rooms warm, and in spite of thick carpet there was always a suspicion of movement beneath one's tread. Besides, Laurence weighed at least a stone more than he should. And according to the bathroom scales he was still putting the pounds on, however much he liked to kid himself otherwise.

Now, above any movements or plods on the stairs, she heard the rain. It was beating against the closed window, and even the double-glazing didn't stop the long red curtains from moving gently in a draught, as if they were breathing.

She had hoped the weather forecast might be wrong, or out in its timing. But the wind sounded as devastating as it had six weeks ago, just before Christmas. Gusts of 90 miles an hour had brought down many of their lovely pine trees – part of the woodland between the house and the adjoining golf course. They had had to be sawn up. It saddened her to think of them with their insides exposed, ring-patterned and pale, stacked discreetly around the far side of the drive behind the shrubs. Now, instead of standing upright and proud, providing windbreak and privacy as they had for years, they looked like jumbo-size sticks of seaside rock, prospective log-cabins, or so much lumber for the sawmills.

Tonight, drivers had been advised to keep off the roads. She wondered if Neville-someone-or-other, and Ian Price, would come after all. She had met Neville once, briefly, in Laurence's office a few months ago. She remembered the smooth baby face, pale blue eyes, high-pitched voice. She hadn't liked him much.

But Ian Price, on the few occasions she had met him briefly, had seemed quite different: tall, good-looking and quietly spoken. Possibly in his mid-thirties, ten years older than she was. She remembered how he seemed more serenely mature than Laurence at forty. According to Laurence, Price played a good round of golf, was terrific on the squash courts, and played second violin in the city's Municipal Orchestra. Those facts had reminded her that when not secretary to Laurence, her own creativity had been taken up with looking after invalid parents and Annaliese. Now, and often with practically no notice, she had to be ready to entertain whichever of Laurence's associates he chose to invite. Many she didn't know, or even want to. But this evening she would, as always, play the perfect hostess. Drawing on what Laurence had told her about Ian Price, she would put on a soft-playing background of Mozart.

She stopped reflecting, and went on to the drawing room. Annaliese was sitting on a settee reading a book. Looking at her, Helena felt she was glancing at her own reflection: the same slanting brown eyes, small tilted nose and neat size 12 figure. Annaliese's shoulder-length hair, the same shade of chestnut as her own, variegated from rich brown to gold in the lights from the well-placed wall-lamps. Helena preferred to wear her own hair short, with a fringe, which at least made her a little different.

They exchanged smiles. Annaliese went on reading. It was usual at this time for Helena to sit down for a few moments before going upstairs. They communicated so easily, often with little need of finger-spelling, lip-reading, gestures or signs, that Helena sometimes forgot there was any difference between them. Even if Annaliese could not walk for miles, she could do practically everything else. She helped in the house, kept her own room clean and tidy, and filled the rest of the time with her sketching or painting, or using her laptop. And she liked to read – when she was not keeping Julie's four-year-old Ben amused, playing his favourite pastime of Noughts and Crosses. In fact, Helena mused, there was little that Annaliese couldn't do. Except speak clearly. And hear the birds sing.

Watching, Helena was mindful it could be herself in that silent world, if she hadn't arrived one hour earlier and escaped the complications that resulted in her twin being injured at birth.

Catching Annaliese's eyes as she looked up, Helena smiled then went upstairs. She heard the wind and the rain. It seemed as if the French windows that opened from their bedroom onto the balcony would at any moment come crashing in. Thunder reverberated and the wind raged. It sounded as if trees were again being wrenched from the ground with splintering, shattering cries. Ridge tiles crashed, chimneys flew, glass shattered. She thought she had just heard a greenhouse crash, or perhaps the conservatory. And for once she was glad that noise couldn't frighten Annaliese.

Still smarting from Laurence's remarks on giving up their home and going to Canada, she prepared to change. Selecting clothes and throwing them onto the bed, she wondered how anyone could be expected to turn up on a night like this.

'Neville's here,' Laurence told her minutes later, as if reading her thoughts. A towel round his waist, a bathrobe over his shoulders, he'd just come in from the shower.

Helena turned. 'Already? He's prompt. I didn't hear.'

'Can't hear anything in this racket. I saw his headlights turn into the drive, I slipped down to let him in. He's in the library.'

She wondered if Laurence was going to say more about Canada. She couldn't stand it just now.

'I told him to come early. Can have a chat. Before Price gets here.' Throwing his robe onto a chair he pulled some scales out from against the wall, dropped his towel onto the floor, and stepped on. Naked, he massaged his slack stomach upwards with his hands, trying to draw it in flat. He stuck out his well-covered ribs, while the needle on the scales swung uncertainly from side to side before jerking to a stop.

He slapped his suspicion of a paunch: 'Not bad, lad, not bad at all.' He paused before proclaiming loudly, 'Twelve stone nine. Not bad, eh?' He stepped off the scales, picked up his towel and threw it over his shoulder.

She said nothing. She knew that he knew that the scales were over seven pounds adrift in his favour, but he wouldn't admit it. She felt, rather than saw him moving around in what he called his side of the room, taking his clothes from the built-in wardrobe with its floor-to-ceiling mirrored doors.

'I can't think why you had to give your sister the other room,' he grumbled lightly. 'She doesn't need all that space.'

'So you're always saying. But this room's plenty big enough for us, Laurie. You know it is.' It was his excuse for another dig at Annaliese. 'She spends a lot of time in hers. There's the view. She can sit in the bay and see right up the fairway.'

'But she's not interested in golf.'

'Perhaps not. But there are people to see. Well, sometimes. And players. And caddies. And all the trees.'

'There won't be many of them left much longer, by the sound of things.'

She reached for the slim-fitting jersey dress she had laid out on the bed. She had always liked it, but especially welcomed its warm comfort on this stormy night. In spite of the central heating the exceptionally high winds seemed to find their way in through minute cracks and crannies of the elegant but rambling old house.

Laurence took it from her hands. 'You don't want to wear that, Helena. You want to look pretty. Put on that blue thing.'

She knew he meant the sleeveless dress with a halter neck, and no back. Protectively she pressed her hands to her lumbar region: 'It's not very warm.'

'Good God, Helena, you don't want to look a frump like your sister – skirt and jumper.'

That was unfair. Any fair-minded person could see Annaliese dressed well to suit whatever the occasion. But to save further unkind comments Helena put the light green jersey back in the wardrobe. Standing in her underclothes, mere scraps of black satin and lace that he persisted in buying, and insisted on her wearing to please him, she took the flimsy blue dress from its satin hanger. It didn't suit her chestnut hair half as well as the green, and she just hoped that as the evening wore on, when Laurence had downed a few whiskies, he wouldn't turn down the central heating.

She stepped into the calf-length blue dress and slipped its halter over her head, leaving her white shoulders bare. At least it seemed he was going to say no more about Canada for the time being; he probably hadn't fully noticed the effect his pronouncement had had on her. He didn't like opposition; didn't expect it. If he had seen her scowl at all, he had probably interpreted it as mere surprise. He had since been quite affable. She was already beginning to feel better about it than she had at first. Later, when she was calmer and they were on their own, she would be able to put her views rationally.

She sat at the dressing table. In the mirror she saw Laurence on the other side of the room frowning at his reflection in the wardrobe door, as if he regretted the way his dark hair was already receding. He adjusted his silk tie, and slipped into a dark jacket. He jerked it by the lapels to sit well on his shoulders, sized himself up, head on one side, and patted his stomach. He looked towards her so that she saw his face above hers in the mirror.

'That's that, then. I'll get down to Neville. You don't want to hurry. Price shouldn't be here for half an hour.'

'Right. See you.' She wondered why it was always 'Price' not Ian. But Neville. Always Neville. She'd never heard his other name.

The sound of the wind made her feel cold. Or was it the scanty blue dress that made her want to hug herself, to rub her arms up and down to improve their circulation, and to blow her nose? She did all three, then applied her make-up with extra care. Her fair skin with nothing added was apt to look too pale in the evening, but a shade too much blusher looked even worse. She liked to get it right.

Downstairs, Laurence closed the library door behind him. He drew a big leather armchair as closely as he could to the one in which Neville lounged cross-legged, affectedly smoking a cigarette in a long black holder.

'Then it's down to business, Neville. Any further bright ideas while I've been upstairs?'

'Nope.' The younger man sat up, leaned forward, and daintily tapped his cigarette ash into an onyx ashtray on a small table. 'He's got a gun. And knives. But you prefer hit-and-run?'

'Cleanest.'

'And hardest to prove it wasn't an accident?'

'Quite. But your Josh – never caught you said.'

'Well, always a first time. 'Course ... use his own car. Something stolen wouldn't help him.'

'Isn't he ever scared?' Laurence spoke in little more than a whisper, in spite of the solid library door firmly closed.

'Not if the money's right. He's a lovely man, is Josh.' Neville blew little rings of smoke that floated towards the high, embossed ceiling.

'I won't supply a photo.'

'He won't want one. Says people don't look the same. He's got a good memory for faces.'

'All right, then. Can I rely on you to do everything?'

'I wouldn't for anyone else.'

Laurence ignored the coy smile. 'Settled then. I'll be in London on business, March twenty-third to the thirtieth.'

'Not till then?' Neville tapped his cigarette again.

'Gives him four weeks to plan; get to know her movements. Memorise her face. The seven days I'm away should provide the opportunity. When it's over . . .'

'Then there won't be anyone here who . . .'

'My secretary will know where I am. I'll expect an urgent call at my hotel. Or at the city office.' He smoothed his thick eyebrows which had a tendency lately to grow towards the bridge of his nose and curve out like pincers. He whispered, 'While I'm waiting to hear the tragic news I'll make sure I'm seen at all times. Much in evidence, in one or other of those places.'

'Can I ring?'

'Keep out of it. No phone calls from you. That's why I asked you here.' He reached for a cigar from a box on the table: 'And just not to seem too tête-à-tête this evening, I've asked Ian Price along, too.'

'The estate agent?'

'You know him?'

'Vaguely. By sight.'

'We do business. Just occasionally. I know it's hardly ethical on a social occasion, but it'll seem like my reason

11

for asking him tonight if I ask him the rough value of this place. I want everyone to know I plan to go with Helena to Canada. Then after the tragedy, my emigration, pre-arranged, won't look like running away.'

'Have you mentioned Canada to Helena?'

'We don't mention names.'

'Sorry.'

'Never. Don't forget. Never.'

'No, Laurie, 'course not. Code name Troy. Helena of Troy,' he giggled.

'I just want her dead. Understand?' He spelled it out. 'D.E.A.D.'

Chapter 2

'How much would a property this size fetch today, Ian?'

Laurence spoke lightly but Helena went cold. She thought it pretty poor taste his talking business however lightly, and so soon, at the dinner table. It was unforgivable. She knew exactly what was going on in his devious mind, she could read him like a large poster.

'Not thinking of selling, are you?' Ian sounded mildly surprised.

Laurence leaned towards him and topped up his tall-stemmed glass with Rioja. 'Wouldn't mind seeing more of the world. Not good to get stuck in a rut, like I'm always telling Helena.' He shrugged. 'I just wondered about the market. Up and down, up and down.' He refilled his own glass and passed the bottle to Neville, who was sitting on his right.

Helena didn't want to hear, detecting clearly what was going on in Laurence's mind, whatever he feigned. He was good at saying one thing while thinking another. But as far as she was concerned, her home with its five bedrooms, two bathrooms, studio, three reception rooms, library, and usual offices, were not for sale.

Laurence went on, 'As you probably know, there's nearly three-quarters of an acre counting the lawns and shrubberies all round. Then there's the woodland between here and the links.'

Ian glanced round the table. 'There's still plenty of money around. I mean for up-market. You'd have no problem.'

Helena liked the way Ian never carried on a one-to-one conversation with Laurence, but looked at each of them around the table as he made his remarks.

He went on, 'Of course, sometimes it's a question of waiting for the right person to come along.'

She was conscious of everything about Ian. Dark hair brushed back from his high, smooth forehead; the neat moustache outlining his good-humoured mouth which belied the tantalising, wicked-landlord image of his sideburns.

He repeated, 'The right person. He'll pay. No quibble if your place is just what he wants.'

His eyes, grey and gentle, sent a bitter sweetness through her, and his rich voice was a pleasant contrast to Neville's. But she didn't want to hear about property and market values. She was afraid Laurence might mention seriously his outrageous suggestion that they emigrate to Canada, and for the sake of good taste she would have to suffer in silence. Perhaps if she showed no interest the discussion might fizzle out.

She glanced round the table to see that everyone had all they wanted. Perhaps Laurence had only broached the subject to note her reaction. He should know by now that however much he provoked her in company, she would never reveal even a hint of the underlying strain between them. If his idea really was to sell up, she hoped he would be too busy for the next hour or so, indulging his favourite hobby of eating and drinking, to discuss it further.

To ease her anxiety she concentrated her thoughts on Neville. He had surely lost weight. The baby face she remembered had almost gone. His eyes, pale blue and deep set, were beginning to hollow. His complexion was still clear and girlish, but she was not sure if the pink flush on his cheekbones was natural, or Elisabeth Arden. Nor if his brown hair was permed. It waved on top, then fell straight to the nape of his neck, and curled around his ears. She passed a small dish of baby carrots to Annaliese, recalling that Neville had worn a brightly flowered shirt in Laurence's office. She rebuked herself for thinking it had at least looked more cheerful than the ghastly white silk polo neck jersey that encased his thin body now. She blamed Laurence for her mood. His complete lack of consideration to consult her on important domestic matters had made her angry, and she felt uncharitable.

'And what do you think, Helena?'

She started. Ian was speaking to her. Reflecting, she had missed the gist of the conversation.

'What would you like to do?'

'Oh, Helena doesn't know,' Laurence answered for her. 'I'm always having to tell Helena what she wants to do.'

She saw Ian's quick glance at Laurence before he looked back at her. His smile disarmed her. Her cheeks burned. What had he thought of that remark? She assumed nonchalance as if she hadn't heard it, and reached for her wine. For a long moment over the rim of her glass, their eyes met.

Laurence said, 'In fact, I don't know what my dear wife does with her time all day.' He helped himself to a second large helping of vegetables, and raised a questioning eyebrow in her direction.

She gave a small smile; their company could think him just a tease, and probably would if she just smiled. She had known for months past, that the sort of things she did all day counted for nothing in Laurence's book. Menial tasks, like running the house, shopping, being able without notice to cater for whoever he chose to invite here to dinner. And by her not mentioning such commitments as keeping Annaliese company, ferrying her to medical appointments, speech therapy sessions, and adult classes at the special school for the deaf, she had learnt not to incite his usual reply, 'Well, if you must, that's your blasted funeral.'

He bantered again in mock wonder, 'Just what do you do with yourself all day, Helena?'

She put down her glass. Smiling, she justified, 'I do social work. There's the WVS and Meals on Wheels.'

Gale-force wind pounded the windows. Heavy rain sounded like gravel being hurled against the glass. 'Well, there'll be plenty for you to do tomorrow by the sound of things.' He looked from one man to the other, a grin on his face. 'My dear wife goes around scrubbing people's homes when they get flooded. I tell her, it's always the same. People shouldn't live by the river.' He laid down his knife and fork. 'Whenever there's some disaster she goes out collecting blankets and parcelling up other people's cast-offs, to send them.' He leaned over the table towards her. 'What you really want, Helena, is a hobby. You shouldn't be wasting your time charring, and driving a little white van, and trotting round to old people with their midday dinners.'

He wiped his mouth with his napkin. 'What you want, Helena, is a hobby,' he repeated, sounding as if he might have had a whisky too many before the meal, as he went on, 'Do something proper. Be creative. Like Neville here. That's what you want.'

Neville giggled. 'Oh I don't know. I can't really say . . .'

'Well, you reckon you're creative, don't you?' Laurence picked up his knife and fork. 'I suppose you think you make people look pretty, or beautiful, or something or other, don't you?'

'Oh well. Yes.'

Helena felt embarrassed. It was the way Laurence spoke. Put people down. The pink on Neville's high cheekbones deepened and spread. His pale lips tweaked. He reminded her of a schoolboy snubbed by the prefect he'd got a crush on.

He simpered, 'But that's my work, Laurence. I do create. Of course. You're right.' He focused solely on Laurence. 'But it takes all my energy. You'd never believe. By five o'clock I feel quite wrung out. Honestly. Limp as a rag.'

Ian showed polite interest, his smile reaching his grey eyes.

Laurence explained, 'Neville dresses ladies' hair.'

'Oh, not just ladies. We're unisex. And I'm standing all day. My poor legs. I'm on them all day long. Except if I'm doing a manicure.'

Helena saw Annaliese was trying to watch Neville's lips, and though she couldn't hear his mellifluously sing-song voice she smiled and chuckled when they all did.

'That's how I met Laurence. Wasn't it, Laurence? Through my work.' He looked at Laurence, who was too busy eating to look up from his plate to reply, so Neville spoke directly to Ian. 'Do you know, there was this woman . . . quite old she was, about fifty, wasn't she, Laurence?'

Helena wished Neville would look at Annaliese sometimes, and move his lips when he was speaking, in the same way as Ian did – instead of never looking at Annaliese, treating her as if she wasn't there.

'Well this woman . . . I tinted her hair. I do tints. Some people call them colourants, but I think tints sounds nicer, don't you? Laurence does.'

Ian listened, but divided his attention. He turned to Annaliese beside him so she could see his lips. 'Wine?'

Before he picked up the bottle, she returned his smile and her brown eyes sparkled. 'Tha . . . nk yooo.'

Neville said, 'Well this woman's hair went green. She was going to sue me. So I went to Laurence, didn't I, Laurence? About six years ago, wasn't it, Laurence?'

Laurence nodded with his mouth full. Helena suspected

Laurence was more interested in his food than recounting claims for hair damage.

'I'd never been to a solicitor before. 'Til Laurence.' Neville paused to resume eating his asparagus, holding it daintily by the tips of his long slender fingers, and dipping its pale head into his tiny side bowl of melted butter.

'The silly woman. She had used something she shouldn't have used on her hair.' He tut-tutted. 'I mean before she came to me. Laurence found that out. Didn't you, Laurence?'

Laurence nodded.

'Goodness knows what would have happened to my reputation if it hadn't been for Laurence. She had no case. Laurence told her, didn't you Laurence? I'd have been taken to court.'

'As I was saying, Helena,' Laurence interrupted, and she cringed inwardly at his rudeness, 'what you want is a hobby. Even if Neville hasn't. There's Price here.' He glanced at Ian. 'What's it you play?'

'The violin.'

'There you are, then. Helena doesn't even play an instrument. Her music's canned. Like this thing she's stuck on for us.'

'Piano Concerto in C major?' Ian sounded appreciative.

Laurence looked blank.

'Mozart. Wolfgang Amadeus,' Ian said.

'You like it?'

'Very relaxing, don't you think? Especially this powerful first movement. Allegro maestoso.'

Laurence grunted. 'Helena calls it background. Always got it on. Get up and stick it off, Helena. You don't want that. We're talking.'

She never argued in company. But now she could just picture Ian playing in the municipal orchestra, in the

18

brocade waistcoat he was wearing tonight, and the black jacket that fitted perfectly on his broad shoulders.

Laurence said, 'Someone told me you're a bell ringer too.'

'Whoever?' Ian chuckled.

'One of your staff, I think.'

'No. Not me.' He glanced round the table. 'But actually Miss Roberts, that is Gail, in the office, she is apparently a dedicated ringer.' He glanced at Laurence. 'Your informant, if it was one of my new girls, was probably confused.'

Laurence raised a thick eyebrow. 'How come, confused?' He grinned, his tone questioning, 'Are you and . . . er . . . this Gail . . .?'

'Good Lord, no.' Ian laughed softly. 'She's nudging forty.'

'So? Many a good tune, as they say . . .'

Helena squirmed. Did he have to be so coarse?

'Nothing like that. I feel a bit sorry for her. Poor old Gail.' He paused to sip his wine. 'She lives on my way to the sports centre. She plays badminton. It's no great shakes for me to pick her up and give her a lift if I'm going to play squash.' He set down his glass. 'And of course, bell ringing. I often give her a lift to the church.'

'You mean St Mark's?'

'It's hardly out of my way if I'm coming to play golf.'

St Mark's was barely 100 yards away. It stood back a little from the wide tree-lined avenue of large, detached houses where The Firs, in its large grounds, was nearest to the links.

'They make a confounded row, those bells,' Laurence said. 'Eight, aren't there?'

'I wouldn't know.'

'Too busy to find out, I expect – doing other things when you and this Gail are together.'

19

'Nothing like that. Actually, she's a bit of a nuisance. At times.'

'In what way, nuisance? Upsets the wife? What's she like?'

'Earnest. Single. But she has technical skills. She's the only one I can really rely on in the office.'

'I meant, to look at,' Laurence said. 'Is she blonde? Brunette? Curves in all the right places?'

Ian shrugged. 'Not to put too fine a point on it, she's rather plain. Poor old Gail. I can't help feeling sorry for her.' He sipped his wine and put down his glass. 'Bit sad. Forty. Still single.'

'And she fancies you?'

Helena took a silent deep breath. Wouldn't Laurence ever give up?

Ian shrugged again. 'I'm married. She knows that as well as anybody.'

Laurence was incredulous. 'And you having a wife puts her off?'

'I wouldn't know.' Ian reached again for his glass. He glanced at Helena. 'As far as I'm concerned, nothing was ever on.'

'But you still have her working for you? And you still give her lifts in your car?' Laurence persisted.

Ian sipped his wine before answering. 'Well, how do you stop doing something you've done for three years? Without hurting?'

Laurence grunted. 'Neville doesn't have our problems. With women.'

Neville giggled. 'Not if you say so.' He tweaked at his hair. 'I have enough problems cutting and styling. Sometimes there's no pleasing, is there, Laurence?'

Helena had wondered what Neville did for a living. She deplored his constant appeal to Laurence to confirm everything, as if Laurence were a hairdresser too. Or were

20

Neville's appeals his way of letting them all know that he and Laurence were chums? And close. But surely, intellectually, they had nothing in common. Even if Laurence had helped him in a lawsuit, that was business. Hardly reason to befriend and meet socially. Oh well, she supposed, that was just Laurence, there was no accounting. She sometimes wished she had her own silent Tinkerbell to fly around and into his mind; so that as a bee collects pollen, his secrets might be brought home to her.

Laurence said, 'Perhaps if your wife came out with you, Ian, she might protect you from unwanted ladies.'

'I know. But it's no good.'

'This is the first time you've actually been able to come here. I've asked you often enough. I hope you've told her, she's always included in my invitations.'

'Yes, of course. Thank you. I always tell her. She's invited to every social function I attend, but it's no use.'

'Damn shame.' Laurence put Neville in the picture. 'Price's wife suffers with ... what's it exactly ... agoraphobia?'

'Well, yes, sort of. It's a nervous thing. She doesn't come out.'

Helena quietly pressed her handkerchief to her nose.

'Not another cold, Helena? Dear me. Always got a blasted cold.'

Smiling, Ian asked, 'Have you? I'm sorry.'

'Very slight.' She was not used to sympathy, and tonight she had paid extra care, and used an inhaler to clear her nasal passages before applying light make-up to reduce the pinkness around her nose.

He said, 'You look charmingly healthy to me.'

She smiled. Laurence never paid compliments or said nice things. He was usually resentful if other people did.

'If she hasn't got a blasted cold, she's got a bad back,'

Laurence said irritably, forgetting they had company. 'God knows why I married her.' He followed his lapse with a chuckle.

I do, she thought. You were in a financial mess. And as your besotted secretary I was too dumb to realise the sudden loss of your wife coincided with your dealing with my parents' generous will.

She got up and took their empty plates and dishes to the sideboard. She brought back an apricot pavlova and a bowl of fruit. Annaliese fetched the cheese board.

Discreetly, Helena rubbed her arms, annoyed to think of her jersey dress upstairs on its hanger. The scanty garments Laurence insisted she wore were insufficient on nights like this. Draughts found every chink in the lofty house, and she envied Annaliese in her long sleeves and sensible underwear.

She cut the pavlova and handed it round.

Neville enthused, 'Oh goody. I adore pavlova. Don't I, Laurence? I never make anything exotic, in my little old flat.'

'Do you live alone?' Helena asked, and saw the pink of his high cheekbones deepen as he said coyly, 'No, with a friend. But he doesn't cook. This looks divine.'

'Julie made it,' Laurence said. 'Nice girl. She used to cook for me and Muriel.' He forked his meringue. 'She's got a youngster. Little Ben.' He glanced at Ian. 'I expect your wife cooks. But how about the garden? I believe you've got a lot round your bungalow.'

'Too much. Orchard mostly. At the back.'

'Sell it, man. You've got a building site.'

'That'd need planning permission.'

'I'd get it for you. Oh yes, yes. No problem,' Laurence emphasised to contradict Ian who, doubting, was shaking his head. 'I'd get it for you. There are ways.' He tapped the side of his nose with his index finger.

'Well, actually, Carol likes the privacy. And then there's my practice.'

'Practice?'

'Of course. I have to. We do quite a few concerts. The Orchestral Society.' Ian put down his fork and wiped his mouth: 'But I always practise well away from the house, where Carol can't hear.'

Helena looked up from her plate.

Ian glanced round at them. His eyes, usually smiling, were serious. 'I have to practise. But I must consider Carol's heads.'

Laurence raised an eyebrow.

Ian enlightened him, 'She has bad heads. Has had them ever since she lost our baby.'

The baby, and Carol's 'heads', were news to Helena. Her heart went out to him. Seeing Laurence nod, with pursed lips implying he understood, she thought: you don't understand. Because you don't understand anything.

Laurence said, 'Make her snap out of it, man. Bring her over next Friday. We'll have dinner again.'

She could see Laurence's mind working; he was anxious to change the subject.

'Thanks, Laurence. But it's no good.'

'Come on your own, then. If she likes being a blasted hermit.'

'Thanks but I couldn't. Not Friday. It's our wedding anniversary. The tenth. Naturally I'll spend it with her at home.'

Poor Ian, Helena thought. A delicate wife. And he's always so kind to everyone. Life's not fair.

They withdrew to the drawing room. It seemed quieter there, on that side of the house. Or perhaps the wind, after intensifying in the early part of the evening, had died just a little.

She served them coffee.

Laurence offered Ian a cigar, then fetched a bottle of whisky and some glasses. Neville managed somehow to produce his own cigarettes from the pocket of his skin-tight trousers. He fitted one into a long black holder.

Over a cup of strong coffee, Helena assessed the evening and asked herself what this particular get-together of Laurence's had been in aid of. Nothing interesting had been discussed. Small talk. Tittle-tattle. Only Ian's presence made it bearable, and even that for her was bittersweet.

She sat listening. At least Annaliese, though she politely refrained from reading her book, was spared Laurence's hard cynicism, and Neville's high-pitched sing-song.

Helena continued her role of hostess for the next hour. But she knew that Laurence, now the catering and niceties were over, would not mind how soon she and Annaliese wished them good night. She got up, smiling. 'Well, gentlemen, Annaliese and I are going to leave you to enjoy your men's talk. I'm sure you'll excuse us. Thank you both very much for coming.'

Neville nodded; his smile hardly reached his deep-set eyes. 'Good night.'

Annaliese went upstairs.

Ian stood up. He walked beside Helena to the door, acting beyond the needs of courtesy, pausing just outside in the wide hall, to thank her for her hospitality and to wish her good night.

He shook her hand. Did she imagine he held it longer and tighter than necessary? For a split second she felt she had consumed champagne, before she came back to earth. Ian was married.

He repeated, 'Good night, Helena.' Then lowering his voice he held her hand more tightly. He raised it and kissed it. 'God bless you, Helena. We all have our crosses.'

Chapter 3

Helena lay awake for hours, Ian's last words running through her mind. It was kind of him to put it like that – 'our crosses'.

She had hoped, though, that by not responding to Laurence's boorishness throughout the evening, she might have helped it to go unnoticed. And she thought she'd hidden the embarrassment he'd caused her by his other lapses of good manners; the interruptions and snubs, the asides and secretive glances exchanged with Neville.

Ian surely could not have meant Annaliese. She was no cross. Or had he meant Laurence versus Annaliese? That was certainly where some of her problems were, but she intended soon, once and for all, to sort them out.

She fell at last into a fitful sleep, and was scarcely awake and refreshed when the phone rang. The WVS needed her help.

Laurence grumbled, 'Didn't I tell you? It's always the blasted same.'

She knew that after breakfast she could leave Annaliese in charge. Annaliese would have the house to herself when Laurence had gone to the office. Julie would not be coming in, so there would be no little Ben pestering Annaliese to play Noughts and Crosses. Annaliese could paint in peace. From her studio window she had done some beautiful pictures of the woods around the links. But lately she had turned her talent to figure drawing, to little Lowry golfers on the fairway, and she was anxious to get on with them. Full of enthusiasm she was gradually bringing them up closer and closer on her canvas until now they were becoming real people, with smiling faces.

Helena opened the large front door to the portico. From between the pillars at the top of the stone steps overlooking the drive she surveyed the damage. Broken glass lay scattered by another fallen tree, and others were now lurching.

She went down. In the garage she slipped into her Mondeo and drove slowly from the curved sweep of the drive out into the wide tree-lined road, careful to avoid fallen branches and twigs, miscellaneous debris, and mounds of gravel washed from she didn't know where by the night's torrential storm.

The rain had stopped now. Sun shone on the night's havoc. But at the other side of the city the river had burst its banks. She found people everywhere – firemen, electricians, Post Office engineers. Bands of students, the Salvation Army, Council officials, and her colleagues in the WVS.

Extra police diverted traffic. Bulldozers were clearing uprooted trees, scattered branches, and lengths of brick wall lain flat but otherwise unbroken, as if they had been made of card. Council workers and troops shovelled mud and rubble, and from doorways people shifted sodden sandbags.

She saw wrecked houses. Muddy, littered water dashing alongside kerbs. Pavements missing. Drowned cats, dogs, little pigs, and rats.

A medical officer toured the devastation. In a corner-shop window appeared a notice: 'Wellingtons in Stock'. In another: 'Opening at 3 p.m.'

From houses where the water had subsided, Helena helped tired, work-worn women bring out mud-sodden floor coverings, and helped to stack them in ever-growing

26

piles along the road. Where there were garden walls left standing, she helped drape rugs and grey carpets.

She saw it was the same in house after house. Indoors, beside open windows overlooking gardens which were no more, sofas and chairs were stacked on tables to catch the mocking sun. But too often furniture, which yesterday had been someone's pride, someone's home, stood mud-stained beyond hope in the road like effects at an auction for which there would be no bid.

Fire pumps and floats and high-wheeled army lorries moved slowly into a side street that still looked like a river. They sent back fresh waves of thick muddy slush into the nearly cleared main road. A small boy, Wellington-deep, played at damming its flow with a cardboard box. The air reeked with disinfectant.

Between fetching and carrying, Helena made countless cups of strong tea for people distressed and disorientated in their own homes. Some recounted their experiences. Others, old and appalled, just looked on. There were few smiles. Outwardly, no tears. But mud. Everlasting, thick, brown, stinking mud. Helena did all she could. It was late afternoon before she stopped to think of anything else.

Going home, she thought of Ian. She knew roughly where he lived – on the city side of St Mark's, up a narrow road on the right, about half a mile down from The Firs. She had never used that road. In spite of its being on the outskirts of the city it was not properly made up, leading as it did to only a few fields and isolated bungalows.

As she drove past she wondered how his trees had fared in the storm. The orchard where, to spare his Carol her bad heads, he went when he wanted to practise playing his violin.

It almost pained her to think he lived so near and yet so far; so loving and considerate for his Carol. She stifled her envy. She had spent all night turning things over in her mind, trying to suppress how she felt about him. She concluded it would be less torment if she could stop having to see him. Better if she did go to Canada with Laurence, providing that Annaliese went too. But first she wanted to know just why Laurence was so suddenly eager to leave here.

A policeman flagged her down, there was a hold-up ahead.

Was Laurence in another financial mess? Like the accusations of fraud that he had been eventually cleared of? Suspect dealings she'd learned about only after she had married him and had left the firm. If so, by going away with him now, would she appear to be involved?

The driver in the car behind her was getting impatient and trying to turn.

She recalled the last time there had been whispers of trouble. Rumours. Mysterious goings-on, and then accusations. Laurence was proved innocent. But she wondered if he had as many friends in high places now as he had then? She didn't think so. Perhaps they thought, as she did, that a solicitor, like Caesar's wife, should be above suspicion.

She was tired. Her back ached. She was sick of worrying about Laurence. She relived the moment when last night Ian's gentle, slate-grey eyes had met hers across the table. She recalled their expression when later he had taken her hand and held it tightly in his, and said with such feeling, 'We all have our crosses.'

It's no use, she told herself, I mustn't think of him. She gripped the steering wheel, and waited for a signal that the road was clear. She was not used to chivalry. He didn't know what his obvious understanding did to her, that it threw her thoughts in turmoil. She supposed that by his comment 'We all have our crosses', he was, with his natural kindness, trying to tell her he understood her unhappy situation with Laurence, and cared.

The policeman waved her on. She eased her foot off the clutch. She didn't want Ian's sympathy. She repressed the dreadful, guilty truth that what she wanted was him. She thought of his fine physique that enabled him to play strenuous squash, hours of golf, and still have energy left for music. Why did some people have everything: good looks, charm and talent, as well as a successful business and, she surmised, a happy marriage?

According to Laurence, it was Ian's good looks and money that made him so popular, especially with women. She ignored Laurence's opinion as typical of him; he was always snide about anyone who had a lot going for them and with whom he couldn't compete. But all the same, she didn't want to have to go on seeing Ian, knowing she meant nothing special to him. He had a wife. He hadn't singled her out, he treated everyone the same – Neville, Annaliese, and even the love-starved Miss Roberts who was apparently so efficient in his office. All received his same courtesy, kindness and consideration.

Especially his wife. The thought of his wife made Helena decide that going to Canada with Laurence offered the best chance of never having to see Ian again.

At home, Helena was surprised to find little Ben with Annaliese. Julie had come after all. Laurence must have asked her, afraid he wouldn't get a proper evening meal if his wife had been out all day. He did that sort of thing without consulting her.

Secretly, she was pleased. She felt lousy. She hadn't thought of herself while she was helping those poor wretched flood victims. Now she was aware her cold was getting worse, and she fumed to think that wearing that thin dress last night hadn't helped her back.

In the sitting room Annaliese was on the sofa, with Ben

on her knees, surrounded by sheets of white paper. A lot had dropped down and were spread around over the carpet. Ben slid down from Annaliese's lap and ran to Helena as she came in. He looked up at her with his soulful blue eyes which rarely blinked, and thrust a piece of paper into her hands.

She appraised it. 'But that's lovely, Ben.' Annaliese had caught his likeness, the round chubby face, the expression in the big eyes.

'That's lovely, Ben,' she repeated, knowing he wouldn't say anything. She wasn't sure if he was painfully shy, or backward for his four years. Tongue-tied with delight he hunched his small shoulders and ran back onto Annaliese's lap and entwined his arms around her neck. Smiling, Annaliese eased away the little clasping hands, and gently slid his feet onto the floor. She stood up, and he understood her words and indication that they should clear up the mess.

From the armchair she had sunk into, Helena watched the little lad's undisguised devotion to Annaliese, noting the eyes that stared with such trust, the chubby cheeks that shone with a seemingly permanent blush, and his short bobbed hair the colour of cornflakes.

She blew her nose. Blasted cold.

She smiled to see Annaliese stacking her retrieved sheets of paper, and Ben watching before he made scrabbling, abortive attempts to make his own pile as tidy as hers. His small collection slipped and fell back onto the floor. In a rising little paddy he grabbed up the recalcitrant pieces in a crumpled heap and thrust them into Helena's keeping.

Smiling to herself she glanced at the sheets of paper, smoothing them out. She recognised the postman, and the milkman, and the girl from speech therapy. She marvelled how quickly Annaliese sketched, mostly from memory, yet still captured a likeness. She turned over several more pages, skipping those that were just Noughts and Crosses, but enjoying Annaliese's faces and figures and the lively-looking pussycats drawn for Ben.

She came to the last picture, and her pleasure of the past few minutes vanished. She froze. As if mesmerised she stared at the portrait that Annaliese had boldly drawn in charcoal. It was not the eyes that held her attention, even though the shading around them was exaggerated and verged on caricature to show they were hollow. Neither was it the hair, perfectly shaded to suggest the wave on top, and the curls around Neville's ears. It was the look in those deep-set eyes, the expression on the face. Something that last night she had seen and felt, and thought she could have only imagined. But Annaliese had seen it. Caught it. Remembered. And put it down. It was the face of *Evil*.

Helena got up and put the sketches onto a side table. She looked at Annaliese, who watched her lips. 'I take it Laurence is home.' She had seen his car in the garage.

'He' . . . s . . . in . . . in . . . the . . . li . . . brary.'

She went to find him, noticing on the way he'd switched off the hall radiators. Petty economies were quite beyond her. It was her money that helped towards bills and subsidised his gambling.

She found him slumped in his leather armchair, beneath a pall of smoke from his freshly-lit Havana.

'Ah, so it's Helena. The Good Samaritan has returned.'

She plonked into a chair beside him. To say she felt ghastly would add fuel for his sarcasm. Instead she queried, 'I see Julie's here?'

'Yes, yes. I guessed you might not be in any hurry to leave your old fogies and get back.' He paused. 'And I've asked two or three from the Club.'

'Oh God no!' she said under her breath.

'I've told her. A leg of lamb. I knew I couldn't rely on you.'

31

She realised she hadn't eaten all day. Yet food was the last thing she felt like. Tired, she wasn't prepared for confrontation either, but this matter was something she had to get sorted out before she would know peace of mind.

'Laurence, I've really come in to know more of what you were saying last night about Canada.'

He didn't reply.

'I was asleep when you came to bed, and I had to dash off this morning.'

He pulled on his cigar and exhaled, making a fog. 'My dear, you don't want to talk about that just now, I've had a big day.'

'But I *do* want to, Laurence. What's happening? Just what is it you are thinking of doing? And why?'

'You don't want to worry your little self.' He sounded almost affectionate.

'Of course I worry. What's it all about?' Strange how he had seemed eager to spread the news to Ian and Neville, and goodness knows who else; but with her, beyond mentioning it at the most inopportune time, he seemed reluctant to discuss it further.

'A new life, Helena. You don't want to stay for ever in a one-horse town. Think wider.' He paused. 'Now. You must show a little consideration. I've told you. I've had a big day.'

She wasn't going to let him sprawl in peace, with his stomach bulging despite the daily pummelling he gave it on the bedroom scales. 'This is a perfectly good city, Laurence. And I've got friends.'

He laughed unpleasantly. 'You think I haven't?'

'Then why? And what about your practice?'

'Everything's being taken care of.'

'And this house? My home?'

'Don't let's have any of that sentimental lark, Helena.' He leaned towards a side table, put his cigar down, and poured himself a whisky. 'We can hold on to it if you like. While we see how things go. Perhaps Price could let it.'

'You haven't said why. Or when.'

'I thought mid-April.'

'God! Not so soon, Laurence, I can't. There'll be masses to do.' She had envisaged that a new life, to break away from Ian, would necessitate upheaval, but barely two months . . . ?

'Everything's tied up, Helena. Taken care of. The practice. Plane tickets. A place to stay while we look around.'

'I've got appointments for Annaliese, well into May.'

'Well, she can keep them.'

'How?'

'My dear Helena, you don't imagine . . .'

She turned hot and cold as he went on, 'I've made enquiries. There's a nice place here. You don't want to start a new life, tied.'

She stood up. 'How dare you!' Her legs shook so, they nearly crumpled beneath her. She sat down again quickly.

'Now Helena, my dear, there's no need for temper. I'll get another air ticket if that's how you feel.'

She felt a pain in her chest. Leaning back against the cushion, she closed her eyes a moment to gather strength before she again faced the self-satisfied grin, the jowl that grew heavier every day.

Recovered, she sat bolt upright. 'I'm *not* going to Canada with you, Laurence! If you go, you go alone. I will *not* leave Annaliese.' She paused, she could hardly get her breath. 'What were you suggesting? Leaving her here in a Home? How dare you!'

She had brooded all night on the possible idea behind his thinking and now, knowing it as fact, her reaction came, thrown at him like a stone while her blood was up. If she had calmed down first as she usually disciplined herself to do, things would have been left unsaid to go on festering.

She saw his uncertainty.

He gulped his whisky and put down his glass. 'Now, don't be silly, Helena. I've said she can come.'

She ignored his silk-smooth tone. Whatever reasons she gave for not wanting to go, they would not be strong enough for him. But he had already said too much. Now, and not for the first time, she didn't trust him. He'd given in too easily. Her head throbbed.

On impulse, she blurted out, 'Laurence. It hasn't worked. Has it? You and me.'

He said nothing, and she couldn't fathom his expression.

'I'd like a separation, Laurence. I suppose, if you go to Canada, well it will be a trial . . .'

He still didn't speak.

'Or I could get it done properly, see someone, I mean a solicitor.'

He sat up straight, his face turned puce. 'And where do you intend to live?'

'Well, here I suppose. For the time being.'

'And what on?'

She had her own money. Investments he had made for her. She didn't need him. 'You know I could manage. Well, for the time being. Until I get something smaller.'

His laugh was unpleasant. 'My dear Helena. You should know better than to rely on investments.'

She began to feel cold again.

His lips curled. 'Investments? They're up and down. They don't all make the returns promised. You should know that.'

'I know mine should be sound.'

He poured himself another whisky. 'We'll talk about it another time. Didn't you hear me tell you, Helena, I've had a very busy day.'

She wasn't going to be fobbed off. 'I know more than

you think. I know that someone used the nest eggs of a hundred investors to fund his gambling spree.'

'Helena! How dare you! Are you suggesting . . . ?' His voice frightened her.

'I know it wasn't you who went to prison for six years after the Fraud Squad moved in. But was it a damn near case of "There but for the grace of God"?'

'Now Helena,' he modified his voice to reason with her. 'Calm down. Don't be hasty. I mean about a solicitor. Think of me. My position.'

'But where's my money?'

'Look. I'm going to London on the twenty-third of March for a week. Think about it till then.' He paused as if giving her kind consideration. 'And if you still feel the same way when I get back . . .'

'But you haven't answered my question. I still want my money. I should have plenty.'

'My dear, you seem to have entirely forgotten all about Black Wednesday and the stock market crash.'

'That's history, you know it. What difference does that make to me?' It hurt her to take a deep breath. 'I don't believe . . . What are you trying to say?'

'To put it bluntly, Helena, if you bloody insist, you and your precious Annaliese haven't the proverbial brass farthing to rub between you.'

She dragged herself up. There was nothing more she could think of to say now, she felt too exhausted. Standing, her legs were like jelly, and her head like a spinning top. She took a step to leave him alone to his smoke and his whisky, but she couldn't see. Everything was going black.

When she opened her eyes, Annaliese was sitting beside the bed. At the foot, their own Doctor Davis was telling Laur-

35

ence his wife had a very nasty chest. She would be all right in a few days. She must rest.

When they had gone, Annaliese stayed. She smoothed Helena's pillows, put tissues handy, and gave her a drink of water, holding the glass steady while Helena sipped.

The bed was warm. So comfy. Resting against the propped-up pillows, Helena closed her eyes. They must have given her something. Like they used to ... Her breathing was easier.

She saw firemen. Big hoses. Pushed and dragged. Bedsteads floating. Drowned cats on muddy pillows. And Ian standing under the trees in his orchard, playing his violin.

Chapter 4

Ian had stayed home that morning after the storm. He was not concerned about a few fallen apple trees. The orchard really belonged only to Carol's cats. Their dishes, whether the food was eaten or not, were mostly forgotten and left to become hidden in time in the long grass, ready to attract rats, and damage rotary blades when periodically he managed to get a man in with a machine to do some tidying up.

But he did want something done promptly about the damage to his roof. He cared a lot for his property. He had had it built to the specification of a place in France, close to the Swiss border, where he had once stayed. He had loved that place with its split-level charm. And although he had not been able to incorporate the view of distant mountains, the rest was the same. Built into the hillside, it looked like a bungalow from the back. From the front, it resembled a house. French doors from two adjacent rooms led onto a large, full-width balcony, beneath which was a double garage, a cellar, and another room. At the side of the building, a flight of cement stairs led from the kitchen down to a paved yard, and a path up and around to the orchard at the back.

Before its completion, he had fondly visualised pots of geraniums on those steps, or on the tiered parapet above the balustrade – vivid splashes of pink and red like those he remembered in Chambéry.

But here he had found flowerpots got knocked over. The only colour, if any, was provided by the teacloths that Carol draped to dry. And on every grey step was a saucer of milk, a bowl of food, and spills that dribbled their disgusting way down to the bottom.

Now, awaiting the arrival of the workmen he had contacted to fix the ridge tiles, he started to tidy the living room. He picked up some newspapers from the floor, and before putting them in a tidy pile, waved them about to disperse the stale smell of fish. He moved bowls of cat food from various parts of the room, and lined them up on one side. It made the place look at least a bit better, should the workmen have any reason to come indoors.

He nearly slipped. There was something on the carpet. He was going to fetch a floor cloth as Carol appeared. He glanced dispassionately at the slight figure, resigned to seeing the grubby pink dressing gown, and the sloppy slippers with their soft backs trodden flat beneath her bare heels. 'Isn't it about time you got dressed, Carol?'

She yawned, distorting her pretty, though pale, face. 'Gosh. That awful, ghastly racket. All night. It's given me a bad head.'

'It won't get better, your staying in a dressing gown all day,' he said patiently.

She ambled to the kitchen and came back with a large tin of sardines and an opener. She put them down on what, before it was dulled and covered in scratch marks, was a fine, polished oak refectory table. He knew she was not used to his being home. Not wanting to interfere, he waited a moment or two. Then, 'Carol, shouldn't you get dressed before feeding the cats? You'll catch a cold, you . . .'

She shrieked, stopping him mid-sentence, and hurled the tin-opener across the room. It crashed into the bookcase, breaking the glass. 'Now see what you've made me go and do. You've made me cut myself!' Shrieking, she held out her finger. 'Look, it's bleeding!'

'Me?' He sighed. 'Oh well, if you say so.' He locked his teeth to keep himself patient. 'I'm sorry. Run it under the tap. I'll find a plaster. If I can.' He rummaged in an untidy drawer.

She gave the finger a quick suck, and waited, supporting it on top of her other hand as if she had at least slashed her wrist.

Towering above her tousled gold head, gently he took her finger and fixed the small plaster he had managed to find beneath a load of junk. 'It's only a nip, Carol. I can hardly see it.'

'It's bleeding!'

'Yes, but nothing much.'

'Oh no? It's all right for you, it's not you it's hurting. It could turn septic.'

'Well, actually, Carol, I really don't know why you've taken to giving sardines to the cats,' he said shortly. 'They don't seem to like them, don't eat them half the time. The oil probably doesn't do them any good. And you're forever spilling it. Look, it's already all down your front.'

She slopped across the room to retrieve the tin-opener.

He said, 'There was a time when you always cooked fresh fish for them.'

'And you said the place stank!'

'Well, it wouldn't have hurt you to open the window sometimes. But that was too much trouble.' Gently he took the tin-opener from her to finish opening the tin himself. 'Why don't you give them the cat food that you used to?'

'And have them die with that dreadful disease?'

'Oh, be reasonable. You can't blame cat food for one reported death.'

'Topaz wasn't at all well last week.'

39

'So I see from the vet's bill.' He paused. 'Was it catching? What about the rest? Sapphire, and Memphis, and Anubis? Isis, and Rosetta?'

She pouted and shrugged. 'Well, Topaz scared me. Her little nose was hot. And she wasn't eating. I asked the vet to come and give them all a check-up.'

'Your cats cost me more than a whole family of kids would.'

She shrieked, 'Beast, you beast!' She thumped his chest with her fists and burst into tears.

Immediately he put his arms around her, and held her tightly. 'I'm sorry, I'm sorry, you know I didn't mean anything.'

'Yes you did, you know you did! Just because I can't have children,' she shouted and began to cry, adding to her sobs with loud howls of misery.

He let go of her and raised his voice to make himself heard above her hysteria, 'Oh not again, Carol, please!' He pushed the opened tin in from the edge of the table and turned away to continue tidying the neglected room. He thought he heard something outside, and paused to listen before saying, 'Anyway, who says you can't have children? The doctor hasn't. You never damn well will if you won't let me near you.'

'I lost my baby, didn't I?' she shouted.

'But Carol, that was nine years ago. Are you going to go on reminding me for ever and ever?'

'You don't know what I suffered,' she shouted at the top of her voice.

'I should do. You've been blaming me for the last nine years.'

'I was in labour for eighteen hours. Eighteen hours I suffered, for nothing, and you begrudge me my cats!'

'Of course I don't, Carol. You know I don't. I do everything I can to make you happy.'

'Well, you've upset me. And I've got a bad head. If you want to do something you can get me a bottle of brandy.'

'Another? But Carol, I brought you in one only yesterday. Where's it gone?'

'It . . . it got broken, didn't it,' she shouted.

'But Carol, you said you broke one last week. Surely you don't expect me to believe . . .' He stopped as the front door bell rang.

'Who's that?' Carol clutched both hands to the neck of her dressing gown. 'I'm not expecting the vet. I won't have anyone else.'

'Don't look so scared. It'll only be men from the roofing firm to fix the roof tiles.'

'Why did you ask them? You know I don't like people here.'

'We're damn lucky to get them,' he said quickly. 'They're doing a favour, they've got a waiting list as long as your arm after last night.'

'Don't bring them in,' she shouted. 'Don't you dare bring anyone in.'

'Don't worry, I won't.' He glanced quickly round the room, conscious of scratched furniture, and trailing fringe and threads pulled by cats' claws from the moquette-covered suite.

He answered the door to two men from the roofing firm and stayed outside to hear what they needed to do. They erected a ladder against the wall on the opposite side of the house from the kitchen. The older man climbed up while the other, a mere boy who gave Ian a hard look, stayed at the bottom. After a preliminary inspection, the older man came down slowly. 'Looks straightforward, guv. Three be missing. But two more looks to be loose. You'd like they fixed while us be about it?'

Ian was glad they'd used their loaf and brought new ridge tiles in their van. He loved buildings, and always had swift

41

attention paid to any structural damage, and necessary outside maintenance.

Indoors, it was a different story. Sadly he had given up worrying that polish was never used in an attempt to cover scratch marks; and accepted that his repeated efforts to stick back wallpaper, shredded above the wainscot, were a waste of time. He left the men to their work.

Indoors, Carol had released her feline children from their sleeping quarters – the cloakroom off the hall. She was making several trips between there, and the parapet outside the kitchen, putting the cats' bedding out to air; six little mattresses from their individual wicker cots, and six coverlets which she had embroidered in different coloured silks with each cat's name.

It was unusual for Ian to be at home during the day. From under a chair in the living room, Sapphire, the Siamese, her small brown face and legs dark against her cream body, regarded him with suspicion in her light blue eyes. A large Persian, ill-named Rosetta, with her long, silky white hair, sat in the doorway looking proud and sulky as she licked her flesh-coloured lips. And two tabbies, Topaz and Isis, one long-haired and brown, the other silver, chased across the room and nearly tripped him over. He was not so adept as Carol at getting out of their way.

He went to fetch a cloth to wipe up the floor, the job he had been about to do before Carol got up. The mess had been added to now; a sticky trail led to the kitchen. He made the cloth wet and soapy. In the living room he scoured the carpet, and with another cloth he rubbed the wet patch to dry it up as much as possible. He was not sure which cat shed its coat so freely. The surrounding carpet was covered in hairs; it could not have been cleaned for ages. He fetched the vacuum cleaner and switched on. The cats bolted.

He was beginning to make some impression on the floor,

revealing a pattern of colour he had almost forgotten, when above the whirring of the machine he thought he heard something. A scream? Carol in another of her tantrums to get his attention? He switched off to listen, but as the whirring died down, he heard nothing. He switched on again. Then he was sure he heard something different above the sound of the cleaner. It came from up on the roof. A knocking. He switched off. Men talking loudly between themselves as they worked? But they seemed to be shouting. Perhaps he was wanted.

It was quicker to go out through the side and look up – the kitchen door was open. He could still hear their voices, but looking up he could not see them. They must be on the other side of the house where they had put their ladder. He hesitated, half turning. The cats' bedding was draped over the parapet where Carol had put it to air. Then he glanced down the concrete stairs. Carol, being pawed by six cats, was lying in a crumpled pink heap at the bottom.

The telephone rang in the CID Operations Room, and Detective Sergeant Roger Mills picked it up. Before he could speak he heard his boss on the line calling from his office on the floor above.

'Inspector Robeson. That you, Roger?'

'Yes, sir.'

What do you know, or any of your lot down there know, about a Mr Ian Price?'

'Rings a bell. Do you mean the estate agent?'

'That's the chap.'

Mills thought a moment. 'Tall, big, dark. Nice looking. Sideburns and a moustache.'

'No, no, Roger, what's he like? I mean, what does he do? He's married. Any other women?'

The DS hesitated before answering. 'Very nice fella I

believe. Far as I know. I've not had actual dealings; not bought a house or anything. What's up?'

'His wife fell down the concrete stairs at the side of their house.'

'Badly hurt? Dead?'

'As the proverbial doornail. I'd hardly be calling else.'

'Suspicious circumstances?'

'The doctor's satisfied there'd been no other blow before death. But naturally he had to report to the Coroner.'

'Then what's the problem, sir?'

'Apparently Price's own doctor is away. A young locum went. He'd never met Price before.'

'Always the same. One's own doctor missing in an emergency,' Mills said from personal experience.

'There was a chap there, working on the roof or something. He said he heard the woman scream. When he got there, Price was at the top of the stairs.'

'You mean the workman implied . . . ?'

'He may not have meant to.'

'He hadn't seen her fall . . . or shoved?'

'No. He had not. But he did say, by way of casual comment, that he'd heard Mrs Price indoors earlier, screaming and shouting.'

'Doesn't prove anything, does it, sir?'

'Bugger all. The youngster probably had far too much to say. But the doctor played safe, he didn't know Price, after all. Passed the remark on to the Coroner.'

'And you want me to make enquiries?'

'Very discreet, Roger. Price is absolutely shattered.'

'An act, sir?'

'Not necessarily. Remorse, perhaps, if nothing else. Knew a chap once who had the one and only barney in his whole married life. Next day his wife was killed in a train crash.'

'Point taken, sir.'

'There are no near neighbours. But he plays in the local orchestra. Belongs to the Golf Club. And the Sports Club.'

'You want me to find out, on the quiet, just what sort of love nest?'

'Someone must know. At least it's on our own patch.'

Sergeant Mills liked to get out of the office. The tall modern CID building on the edge of the city, was all right if you liked concrete edifices, but he preferred mixing with the public to spending too many hours at a stretch within four walls. Observing and listening to people gave him the zest that made him feel he was going somewhere. At 32, happily married and looking forward to starting a family, he did not intend to remain a sergeant all his life.

He enjoyed playing his own particular game of finding out what he wanted to know – by never seeming to have asked a question. He had friends, who had friends, who had friends. It was amazing how people opened up when they did not realise the topic of conversation was one that you had gently, but deliberately, engendered; and when they were quite unaware that everything they said was being noted, sifted and mentally tabbed. To further his game he joined, or at least took some interest in, as many local activities as he could, if only so that he could sometimes poke his nose into them. He was a member of the local Sports Club, with a card to prove it; even though he almost never had time to use the facilities offered.

Now he perched himself on a high stool, sideways on at the end of the bar, looking reasonably anonymous in his light grey trousers, open-neck shirt, and a casual check jacket.

Roger remembered the barman; a talkative type who knew a lot of members by name. But Roger's was not a familiar face; he had patronised the bar only a couple of times before, and always kept a low profile. Now he ordered a light ale. Some customers carried their drinks to a table; others stayed at the bar to chat with whoever would join them. Roger listened, contributing no more than an occasional grin. He watched the tables being gradually taken. Bare-legged females in minuscule white pleated skirts, trainers, and sports shirts seemed to have segregated from the muscular, hairy-legged fraternity who sweated to the bar, pullovers round their athletic shoulders, or tied about their haunches to look like mudflaps.

News had already broken that Ian Price's wife had had a fatal accident.

'Such a terribly nice man,' the barman said, sliding a glass of lager towards a customer. 'Poor devil.'

'I didn't know his wife,' another man put in.

'Seems not many people did,' the barman said. 'I believe she was delicate. Shy or something. But him ... you couldn't meet a nicer fella.'

'Damn good squash player,' someone said.

'What about that woman he always brings with him? Plays badminton.'

Mills pricked up his ears. A man about his own age was speaking from the other end of the counter.

'Isn't she called Gail someone-or-other? Has she heard?'

The barman, polishing a glass, pursed his lips in a silent: 'Ssh ...', and directed his eyes over their heads and sideways, indicating she was in the room.

No one turned. A fleeting silence fell, broken as two drinkers moved away. Roger would not appear interested, but wanting to hear more he ordered another drink which he didn't really want, and edged towards the man who had spoken. Another drink would make him a trifle disconsolate; his beloved Kirsty had no idea how this job played hell with his resolutions.

More drinkers at the bar drifted away. Others took their place. Roger, contemplating the amber liquid in front of him, more with sorrow than pleasurable anticipation, was alerted by the barman's tone. 'Hallo, Miss . . . er . . . Gail, isn't it? How are you? You've heard, of course? About your friend's wife? I'm terribly sorry.'

'It's Miss Roberts, actually. 'Course I've heard. I was nearly the first.'

Roger, without moving his head, glanced to see who had sounded so haughtily indifferent.

'Lemon and lime,' she said, sliding her money across.

Roger concentrated on his glass.

With a pop, the barman pulled the ring from a can of proprietary lemonade, poured it into a tall glass and added a dash of lime. He put it on the counter in front of her, and gave her some change. He sounded less confident as he asked, 'How's he taking it, do you know?'

'I'll have some ice if you don't mind,' she said, as if she were being cheated.

He tonged three cubes of ice from a chunky little barrel on the counter and dropped them chinking into her glass. 'Have you seen him?'

'I will. Soon I expect. Of course.' She picked up her glass. 'He's not been to the office today. I had to come on the bus.'

While she was speaking, Roger did a casual half-swing on his stool, as if taking in the general view of the large room with its floor-to-ceiling windows that overlooked the indoor swimming pool. Without having appeared to do so, he wanted to watch her carry the drink back to her table. Even from her back view, by the way she held her head, he fancied she stuck her nose in the air. He turned back to the counter.

The barman was polishing a tumbler, and caught his eye. 'Doesn't half fancy herself, that one.'

47

Roger grinned, and made no comment.

'Can't afford to, with her looks.' The barman scrutinised the sparkling tumbler for smears against the light. 'That hair,' he said between his teeth, 'it's dyed I reckon. 'Twould never be so black else.' He tutted. 'And dead straight. These days. With a fringe. Who does she think she looks like? Cleopatra?' He hung the glass upside down from the fitment above his head. 'She's got a bloody hope.'

Roger sipped his ale; he was the barman's only confidant still left at his end of the counter.

'And she's slightly bow-legged. Did you notice? You'd think she'd keep 'em covered up, 'specially when they're as pale as slugs.'

Roger put down his glass and delved into his pocket. 'Think I'll have a packet of crisps, please.' He tendered 50 pence.

'Salt 'n' vinegar?'

'They'll do.'

The man dropped a crackly bag in front of him, and slid over some change from the till. 'Price buys her a drink sometimes. It's gin and tonic then, or even a liqueur for Lady Muck.' He tutted and raised his eyes to the canopy of tankards above him. 'She doesn't choose lemon and lime when he's paying.'

Roger stabbed the tough bag with a fork from a jar on the counter, to get at his crisps.

The barman said, 'Mind, I think it's only when he wants a drink himself. And she's ready to go home.' He wrapped a clean white cloth round his hand and twirled it round inside another glass. 'But she'd like us to think she's his bit of stuff.' He glanced to see there was no one waiting to be served. 'If he wanted a bit on the side, he'd do better than that. Especially with his looks.'

Roger crunched. He liked crisps, but you did not get many in a bag.

The barman said, 'I think to myself, you don't have to buy her a drink, mate. It's you who's going to give her a lift. Let her damn well wait.'

Roger dipped into a dish of salted peanuts on the counter.

'But no, he wouldn't let her just sit there. He's too nice a fella for that.' He paused. 'But Madam . . .' He blew out his lips. 'Acts like a fifteen-year-old when she's with him. Must be forty if she's a day.' He moved away to serve.

Roger got down from his stool. He strolled over to one of the big windows and looked into the bright blue swimming pool. A muscular young lifeguard in the briefest of red trunks patrolled the slippery wet sides, and for his trouble received the occasional splash from those swimming, laughing, shouting and diving. It looked fun. He should come sometimes. Bring Kirsty. But there never seemed time; and she might not want to come with him when she got too pregnant.

He threaded his way out through the tables. He had learnt that Ian Price was apparently a thoroughly nice guy. But his home life remained a closed book. It was the same story wherever he wormed his innocent way. A friend of a friend of his knew Price at the Golf Club. Everyone liked him. Reliable. Good player: had a single-figure handicap. There was no reason to suppose he was not happily married. His wife did not come with him to any of their social events, but not all the wives did. Anyway, she was apparently a bit of an invalid. Had migraines.

Ian Price, it seemed, was also about the most popular person in the local orchestra. Apart from his high standard of playing as second violin, he had a rich tenor voice, and often sang solo. He was reliable, and always ready to bring anyone along to practice, or concerts, if they did not have their own transport. Everyone who had heard he had lost his wife, and in such tragic circumstances, was deeply shocked.

49

Roger made his reports. He handed them to Detective Chief Inspector Robeson in his office, pulled a chair out from under the other side of the desk, and sat down. The reports were not long, and quite straightforward. As the Inspector read them, Roger noted his dark, restless eyes, and the lock of curly brown hair that fell onto his broad forehead. He was aware that his well-built boss, in his late forties, was still as sharp as a finely honed cut-throat razor, with the added advantage of years of experience.

After a few minutes, the Inspector looked up. 'It all fits, Roger. But we had to check up after that workman's remarks.'

'Yes, sir. Price sounds a nice guy.'

Robeson said, 'Apparently the woman had thrown a tantrum earlier. Price admitted it. Told the doctor before she was taken away.' He slid Roger's file back to him. 'She'd cut herself opening a tin of sardines. Price put a plaster on it.'

'What did they make of things at the morgue, sir?'

'The plaster had been applied before death. The pathologist found a blood stain. Her group.' He paused. 'Forensic reported oil on the soles of the woman's slippers. Fish oil. Well, that muck you get in the tins. And traces of the same on her hands. And on the stairs.'

'It's all wrapped up, then?'

'I'd say so. Coroner's got all the reports.'

It surprised no one that five days later, at the inquest into the death of Ian Price's wife, after the Coroner's summing up, the verdict returned was 'Accidental death'.

Chapter 5

'Pull yourself together, Helena.' Laurence dragged the scales from against the bedroom wall and stepped on: 'I could have told you the news a week ago. But I considered your bit of a cold.'

She had merely given a small gasp when, preening himself naked in front of the wardrobe mirror he had said, almost as an afterthought, that Price's wife had died after a fall. Then she had covered her face with her hands just for a moment, before leaning back against her propped-up pillows.

He massaged his stomach, pressing it in as he looked down to see where the arrow on the scales was going to point when it stopped swinging. 'Ah ha! Not bad, lad. Not bad at all.' His mind had already moved on. 'Barely twelve stone ten.' He turned with a self-satisfied grin. 'Not bad, eh, Helena? Oh, don't start snivelling.'

She was about to blow her nose after yet another sneeze, far too stunned for mere tears; the full meaning of Ian's tragic loss had not sunk in. She could not believe it.

Laurence reached for his pants. 'I've let you make a fuss of yourself. All this time. But you can get up today, the doctor said.' He padded across the carpet, put on his shirt, and selected a red silk tie. 'You can write to Price if you like. Give you something to do.' He fiddled in front of the mirror, trying to make the tie set just right. 'You'll want something to do with yourself. Say we heard of his bereave-ment, and we're sorry.' He took his charcoal-grey business suit from the wardrobe. 'You could ask him to dinner on Friday. Yes. Good idea. He's free now, nothing to stop him. He'd enjoy that.'

She felt that condolence, without an invitation, would have been better sent immediately after the tragedy, not after such a delay, when Ian may be trying to come to terms with it. But such communications had always been her lot, and until today she had been too ill for Laurence to have thrust a pen into her hand.

Later, when Laurence had gone to the office, she dressed slowly. Her legs still felt weak, but Julie had agreed to come in every day.

In the sitting room, Annaliese and Ben had been playing Noughts and Crosses. Now she was teaching him to read. She had drawn an apple with a large letter A beside it. She pointed to the picture and sounded the letter A, and the word 'apple', as clearly as she was able. She took a real apple from a crystal fruit bowl on the table and held it up.

Ben repeated the word after her and pointed at the fruit.

Next, she indicated the same big capital A. 'A, is fffoor Aaa . . . na . . . leese.'

Helena wished Annaliese could hear how clearly he had managed it, but guessed she had seen the little white teeth clenched as he had concentrated on the second syllable.

'Aan . . . leese,' he repeated proudly.

It had obviously been hard work for both. Ben had had enough. He thrust more paper at Annaliese: 'Play Crosses.'

Outside, there was a cold March wind. Trees swayed beneath the colourless sky. But in here it was warm, the radiators turned right up. Annaliese had seen to that.

Helena sat down with some writing things in an easy chair, and drew a cantilever table over her knees to rest them on. What could she say to Ian that would not be pathetically inadequate?

'Laurence and I' . . . It sounded so cold and stilted; as if she were the Queen speaking on Prince Philip's behalf. She simply wanted to cry, 'Oh Ian, I am so terribly, terribly sorry, so terribly, terribly sorry.' But what would that look like on paper? Words. Just words. How did you convey the depth of feeling behind them: her desire to hug him, take his hand firmly in hers, to try to comfort him for life's unfairness?

She had no intention of being false, by way of convention – 'Laurence is deeply shocked and thinking of you.' His insensitive remarks earlier had given her full measure of the depth of his sympathy. It was she who was really thinking of him, praying for him in his awful loss. But she did not want to say something that might be misunderstood, sound presumptuous or cheap, or that could detract from any possible comfort that she intended, and which might even put her down in his estimation.

After several attempts, she wrote, 'Dear Ian, I can't find the right words to tell you how sorry I am. But please, if there is anything at all that I can possibly do, please let me know. Helena.'

She folded the headed notepaper carefully, put it in an envelope and sealed it.

Smiling, Annaliese held out her hand. 'I . . . w . . . i . . . ll p . . . post it.'

There was a post box nearby; but even in this reasonably quiet road that did not get much traffic, Helena knew it was not safe for Annaliese to go out alone: 'No no, Julie will,' she said, shaking her head. Getting up, she wondered if the letter was so short that it might seem curt. Did it sound stupid? It was how she felt from her heart.

She had not invited him to dinner. Laurence's idea to

include a social occasion with their commiserations had jarred with her sense of propriety. But after she had given the letter to Julie, she realised she had not even mentioned Laurence. Perhaps she should have stuck to the conventional condolences, stiff and hackneyed phrases among which 'sorry to hear' lost its meaning.

It was too late now. She had been impulsive; acted on her grandma's adage at such times 'A little help is worth a deal of sympathy'. But had she been presumptuous? How could she help? For certain, Ian had relatives who would have descended upon him from somewhere, rallied to help him with all the consequent domestic upheaval after the tragedy, and to give him what comfort he needed.

She thought no more of her note. Two mornings later, having coffee with Annaliese, she got up to answer the phone.

'Helena?'

She was surprised by Ian's tentative inflection. 'Speaking.'

'I just wanted to say, thank you so much.'

She floundered: 'Oh, thank you.' Oh God, how stupid, thanking him for thanking her, but he sounded so gentle, the way he spoke her name.

'Trust you, Helena, to offer help.'

'But surely, yes, of course.' Her confidence returned, at least she had not offended.

'Oh yes. Everyone's been wonderful. I'm so grateful. My sister came from up north.'

How nice of him to ring when she was not even needed.

'Yes, I've had all kinds of help.' He paused. 'But I'm greedy, Helena. I would like yours, too. That you offered.'

Her heart missed a beat. 'Of course. If there is anything I can do,' she assured him quickly and suddenly hoped there'd be nothing too strenuous; in her pleasure and surprise to hear him, she had momentarily forgotten her present physical weakness.

He hesitated before saying, 'I'd like to talk.'

She waited. There must be more.

'Just talk. I feel only someone like you would understand, but I wouldn't want to impose on your kindness.'

'You wouldn't. I'd be pleased to.'

'I loved my wife. But the silly old world goes on.'

'Of course.' It was all she could think of to say; so inadequate, but better than uttering the wrong platitudes.

'I wouldn't want to bore you. You're so patient. I thought just a few words, like this, say, each working morning.'

She presumed he meant during office hours and when Laurence was out. It would give her more pleasure than it could possibly give him. Closing her eyes, she thought, every working morning, for a few minutes, I will be his therapeutic shoulder to lean on.

'Until tomorrow, then.' Ian replaced the receiver.

He looked up. Miss Roberts was waiting beside him with a cup of coffee. Why couldn't she just put it down on the desk, and go? There was enough room; she had already cleared off some of his papers to make way for a bowl of early daffodils, and a tall vase of hothouse carnations.

'Thanks.' He avoided her eyes. She had put fresh flowers on his desk every day for the past year. He had thought that, given no encouragement, she would soon stop. But since he had lost Carol, Gail's floral arrangements were embarrassingly more lavish. He should tell her he wanted no more sympathy, but perhaps she would be hurt.

He had let a lot of business slide during the past two weeks. Now he rallied to his own sentiment that the silly old world goes on. He drank his coffee. Like a genie Miss Roberts materialised from nowhere to remove his empty cup. He asked her, as he took some typed leaflets from his top drawer, 'Who's responsible for these, Gail?'

She put her head of short black hair close to his and looked over his shoulder. 'Oh. The new typist.'

'They're full of misplaced adjectives: "A charming gentleman's detached residence".'

She rubbed her shoulder against his.

He eased away. 'As silly as offering for sale, a second-hand boy's bike. It won't do. Tell her.'

She took them in her free hand.

'However charming the gentleman might be, tell her to alter that to "gentleman's charming detached residence".'

'Of course. I will. Immediately.'

'Second thoughts – just "charming detached residence".' He selected another: 'There's this one, and this – I've marked them where they need rephrasing.' He read another. 'And I'm quite sure we don't have an "almost new gentleman's bungalow" for sale.'

'Oh yes,' Gail corrected him.

He looked up. Her eyes were small, and brown, and unfortunately very close together. 'The bungalow belongs to an almost new gentleman, does it?'

He expected her to smile but she did not, obviously annoyed to be caught out, having appointed herself in the outer office as captain of the ship.

He said, 'An almost new bungalow. The present owner being a gentleman, adds nothing to its market value. So leave him out altogether.'

'Yes, of course, I'll get that done. Immediately.' She retreated with his cup. She was back within minutes, and fiddling round his desk, rearranging flowers.

'Yes, Gail, what is it?'

She came to his side of the desk and stood beside him: 'I was wondering . . . you being lonely now . . . I . . . we could meet more often.'

He was momentarily thrown: 'More often? I didn't realise we ever *met*, as you put it.'

She smiled coyly, twisting her shoulders in a way he assumed was meant to arouse him: 'Bell ringing. And badminton. Those cosy drinks after.'

'I give you lifts if I'm going your way.'

'And I was wondering about the cats.'

'Cats?' He removed her hand from where she had put it on his shoulder.

She tried unsuccessfully to hang on to his fingers. 'You told me once you had cats.'

'Yes, we, I mean I, do have cats. Six in fact. But what's that . . . ?'

'I could come and feed them.'

'I can manage them perfectly, thank you, Gail. Now, if you don't mind, we both have work.' He noticed, for the first time, her unsuitably low-cut blouse. It had little cleavage to reveal, if that was her intention; it merely emphasised the saltcellars above her collarbones.

'My brother can make cat-flaps. He's home from Africa.'

'Thank you, Gail. But I've all the amenities I need. Now I know you've got work to do. You must leave me to get on with mine.' He pretended not to see the pout as she flounced off.

Actually, only at first had the cats been a problem. They had ignored him, and all food, until they had eventually succumbed to hunger and greed, and were over their initial fretting. It had not taken very much to have them chasing around the house again, and clawing the chairs – just saucepans of boiled cod, carefully boned, and bowls of fresh milk. And later, to discourage any prolonged torpor, a few table tennis balls had provided diversion.

So much for devotion. And grief. Just blot it out. Almost anything could be obliterated – carnal thoughts, impossible fantasies, domestic misery. Just expunge them with diversions.

He looked at the phone in its cradle. If anyone had

reason to seek diversion, it was long-suffering Helena, so obviously vulnerable. He would not take advantage. But the thought of Helena lifted his spirits. He breathed, 'I'm sorry, Carol.'

The third week of March started mild; a welcome relief from the recent cold wind, and the gales that had savaged the trees before Christmas and again barely a month ago.

The balmy air tempted Helena out for the first time since her illness, and added to her sense of well-being. She went down the front steps from the portico. The big iron gates to the road were fixed open as usual; Laurence liked to be able to drive in and out without having to stop and get out of his car to, as he put it, 'fiddle with things'. She would prefer the gates kept shut. The open gateway encouraged car drivers to reverse in to turn round when, new to the area, they discovered the road ended just beyond – at the entrance to the golf links.

She had noticed from the drawing room window, that one particular car had crawled by here several times lately. The driver, his face half hidden, had admittedly not reversed in; instead he had backed along the road, but each time he reached the entrance to The Firs he had braked and looked in. She did not like it.

Perhaps he had wanted to admire the camellias that bordered the drive: bushy shrubs loaded with rich red blooms alongside ones covered with showy white blossoms, and set against the lovely gloss of their evergreen leaves. But you did not need to wear large dark glasses for that.

Someone had once told her that mixing red flowers with a bunch of white ones foretold death. There was no end to old wives' tales.

She crossed the drive to walk behind the shrubs, and

along the path that ran between them and the plantation of fir trees on the golf links side. It was so peaceful. Almost hidden from the house, behind the bushes and under the trees, she smelled the sweet scent of pines, felt the soft tread of their needles beneath her feet.

The road entrance to the path was a small garden door marked 'Tradesmen', situated a little further down from the main gate. But those days were over. The postman came up the steps to the front door. The milkman left his bottles at the top or the foot of the steps, according to whim. Now, only Julie and little Ben used the wooden side door.

The path followed for some distance, providing an interesting walk that eventually brought you out on the links, if you were not needing to go just round to the back of the house or to the kitchen. But today Helena lingered where she was, along the path near the side gate, breathing deeply the clear spring air.

It was sad that so many trees had come down in the Christmas gale; their sawn-up trunks were piled behind the shrubs, just inside the gate, waiting to be taken away.

So much to be done and more to think about. Only this morning had she felt strong enough to ask Laurence to explain what he had been telling her just before she was taken ill. How had she incurred such financial loss? What had happened to the sound investments he was supposed to have made for her with her parents' legacies?

'My dear Helena,' he had said, 'you don't want to worry your pretty little head about money.'

She had reminded him, 'But you said I hadn't any, Laurence, when I suggested we separate.'

'That was all a mistake. I work too hard. You know me. Forget it. 'Course your money's sound.'

She felt relieved, though not entirely satisfied, not sure if she could rely on him, and doubtful how long his improved mood would last. It was hard to believe he cared; perhaps he thought their staying together was preferable to having his private life exposed to others in his profession.

He had sounded quite congenial when he had said, 'And don't do any thing silly, Helena. Like seeing anyone about a separation. Promise.' Still pleasantly, as if confident she would change her mind, he had added, 'Think things over. While I'm in London.'

She had felt better after finding him in a less belligerent mood. Now she glanced at the felled trees, surprised to notice that their exposed annual rings glistened with what she supposed were globules of dew. But how like tears they looked, as if the pines were actually crying, sobbing their hearts out for their fate since that December night's fury. She reached out to touch them gently, as if to symbolically dry their tears. But the droplets were not wet; just sticky tears of weeping resin. Thoughtfully, she wiped her fingers then glanced at her watch.

Five minutes later she was indoors, ready and waiting for Ian to ring. She would hear little different from the few words he had said each working day for the past two weeks. 'How are you Helena? You never told me you'd been ill. And Laurence didn't either. He could have. But I heard.' A pause. Then, 'Take care.' A few minutes about nothing. But her daily boost of sunshine. A taste of mead. She wondered if he would talk longer if Miss Roberts did not always arrive with his coffee. His getaway had become predictable: 'Well, I mustn't impose on your time. Coffee's up. Then it's back to the grindstone.'

Everything was predictable. Ian's consideration about her time. Laurence's going to the office nine till five. Annaliese sketching. Or painting, before going down the front steps and across the drive to the prize camellias that thrived in the woodland soil of her favourite walk. And every day, she herself arranging her life around an expected phone call.

It came now. She picked up the receiver: 'Hello?'

'Hello. How are you, Helena?'

'Just fine now.' As usual, a couple of minutes of inanities – how's this, how's that. Even remarks on the weather. 'But how are *you*, Ian?' It was him, after all, who was supposed to be helped by 'just talking'. She waited several moments.

'All the better ... I can't tell you how much, for just hearing you.'

She knew sincerity when she heard it.

'Your voice, Helena. Believe me. It's very soothing.'

She heard a familiar rattle in the background.

'Oh well, I mustn't impose on your time. It seems coffee's up. I'd better drink it while it's hot. Or Gail will be cross.'

The phone rang again about seven. Helena picked up the receiver in the hall. She recognised the excitable high-pitched voice that had not waited for her to speak.

'Laurie?'

'One moment. I'll get him.' She went into the library where Laurence was enjoying a cigar before dinner.

Laurence almost jumped from his deep armchair. 'Neville?' He managed to speak calmly, 'I'll take it here,' he said, reaching for the phone on the table near him. 'Neville? How nice ...' he began slowly, then put the receiver down and got up to make sure Helena had really left and had closed the door behind her. He came back, snatched up the receiver, and hissed, 'What the bloody hell?'

'Code Troy, Laurie.'

'Bloody hell. Told you. Never here!'

'It's Josh, Laurie. Edgy. Cruises. But Troy. No peek. What's up?'

'Been ill.' Laurie spoke as low as was audible. 'Hold on.' He left the room to satisfy himself that Helena was busy in the kitchen, seeing to dinner. He came back.

'All tied up I thought.'

'But scrapped?'

'Hell why?' Laurence snapped.

'You said ill.'

'Over. But I lost my temper. Rash moment. I let out, money blown.'

'Troy *knows*?'

'I straightened the record. Said I was fooling.'

'Josh goes ahead, then?'

'Before little pigs use ears, and hear the trough's empty after all.' He spoke in undertones despite knowing that Helena was not usually interested in his friends or their conversations. 'I'm off on Saturday. Be waiting to hear when I'm well away.'

'Sure, Laurie. Josh won't waste time. Code Troy. D.E.A.D.'

Helena's Saturday mornings were mostly the same. Menial tasks. Laurence was always at home, and Annaliese kept out of his way. Lately, weather permitting, she would go for her favourite walk along the camellia path and around to the side of the golf links. And by midday, the quietness of the wide tree-lined road of detached houses would be broken by the bells of St Mark's Church, pealing for a wedding, or bell-practice, or a visiting band of ringers. Helena felt that today was going to be a little different. To begin with, Laurence was meant to be leaving first thing for London. But he had raised the bonnet of his Rover and peered inside, not too pleased with something: 'I'd better run it into the garage, let them have a look.'

'Anything much? Think it'll take long?' She felt able to ask, as he had been so amiable towards her this past few days. Usually if she'd asked anything, he would have bitten her head off.

He looked at his watch. 'I should've been well away before now. Probably only a twenty-minute job. But you know mechanics.' He shut the bonnet. 'I'm thinking of lunch. Could be rather late for the hotel where I usually stop on the way.'

'Then come back here. Set off after.'

It was a nice day for driving. Or walking. Or anything, she mused. The sort of early spring day that made you feel good; no sign of rain, a soft breeze, and downy white clouds that moved imperceptibly across a pale blue sky. She went to the kitchen. Laurence would not want to be kept waiting for lunch when he got back from the garage.

First she made coffee and took a cup to the sitting room for Annaliese to have before going out for her customary walk. Back in the kitchen she slipped a cassette into her player, then set about peeling potatoes to a background of Mozart's Piano Concerto in C major. When it finished playing she would rewind the cassette and play it again. And again, and again, reminded of Ian. Did he play his violin in the house now? Or was he too shattered to play at all?

She prepared carrots, and Brussels sprouts. Then she trimmed the fat from some lamb chops, and seasoned them ready for grilling. Laurence's idea of lunch was a hearty meal which you happened to consume midday – in his case, as well as in the evening.

She glanced out of the window at the rear lawns, at the circle of trees that stood like sentries between them and what lay beyond. The room became hot and steamy. She shut the kitchen door so that the smell of cooking did not escape into the front of the house. Opening the window, she heard the pealing of the church bells. A nice day for someone's wedding. She liked the sound, but just now it would spoil her Mozart. She closed the window to within a fraction for ventilation, and turned up the volume of her cassette.

Everything was nearly ready. However much hurry Laurence was in, he would not expect to eat in the kitchen as she and Annaliese occasionally did when they were on their own. Today, Annaliese would lay the table in the dining room. But she had not come in; had probably forgotten Laurence would be in to a cooked midday meal. Helena laid the table herself. In the kitchen, she glanced at the wall clock. Ten minutes to one. She supposed Laurence had had to wait for a mechanic, or the car needed more attention than he had thought. He would be hopping mad. He always liked to reach his London hotel before dark, and the journey took at least four hours.

His meal was ready, keeping hot. Annaliese had been gone a long time. Impatient, Helena went through the hall, and as she opened the front door Laurence's car turned into the drive. He braked suddenly and got out.

For a second she stood transfixed, unable to believe her eyes. Annaliese had fallen and was lying face down on the ground. Helena raced down the steps to help her up, but the arm she placed across her back became covered in blood. Cold, disbelieving, gulping back vomit, she raised agonised eyes to Laurence, standing paper-white, looking down. 'Quickly, quickly, the doctor. Hurry, hurry, for God's sake hurry.' She tried not to be sick. As he hustled to the phone she still appealed, 'Hurry, hurry, for God's sake hurry.' Waiting, she moaned on, 'Hurry, hurry, hurry . . .' But she knew it was too late.

Annaliese was dead.

Chapter 6

Early Saturday was usually a quiet time for Detective Chief Inspector Robeson. Later in the day, if the city's football team was playing at home, an army of PCs and officers did extra duty. Luckily, the CID rarely needed to be involved, usually only called in when someone had used a knife, or someone had been killed.

On Saturday evenings uniformed and plain-clothes officers patrolled the roughest areas, equipped with radios to call up extra help if needed. But Saturday, midday, in full daylight, in the open, wide drive fronting a large house in the classiest part of the city, was not, in the normal run of things, the most likely time and place for murder.

Robeson took three phone calls in quick succession. He expected another as he waited in his office on the third floor of Divisional Headquarters. It came within minutes. He snatched up the receiver to hear his immediate boss, Detective Superintendent John Moore, on the line.

'I'm leading the murder hunt, Howard. Scrap any plans you've made for the weekend.'

'Hell!' Robeson exploded. He had been half expecting the news, but until it actually came there was still a chance he could stick to the arrangements he had made. He added quickly, 'Sorry, sir. Of course. Will do. I was looking forward to a few hours with the bird-watching group on the Dray Estuary.'

'Well if it's any consolation, my plans are busted too, Howard.' Moore added bitterly, 'Such as they were, when you've been left to live by your bloody self.' He still blamed the Force for his broken marriage: 'But you know as well as I do, in the CID we can never be sure of a minute to call entirely our own.'

'Aye, sir. And at least this case seems bang on our own doorstep.' Might get home at reasonable times, he told himself. Janet would appreciate that.

Moore said, 'The pathologist has examined the body at the scene. It's been removed to the morgue for PM.'

'Photos, sir?'

'Naturally. SOC officer first there. Cameras, tripod, murder bag, the lot, after the call came from our uniformed lads.'

'What're we dealing with, a stray rifle?'

'Too early, Howard. No reports from forensic. The murder room's jacked up. I've cranked up the machinery of investigation. You know the drill.'

'Aye,' Robeson had played his part in organising the police circus: house-to-house teams, the command team, the search team and the suspects team. And more teams of detectives to control, collate and sift information as it came in. He prided himself that man management was one of his strong points. He liked to have a good working relationship with his officers, be conversant with some of their personal problems, to understand them, and to know which men worked well together.

Moore said, 'Haven't found the weapon. But inch-by-inch search of the drive is already on. I take it you know The Firs?'

'Where Bray the solicitor lives? Largish detached house. Surrounded by trees and hedges, next to the golf links.'

'All detached up there, they lie back from the road in

their own grounds. The residents probably never see their neighbours.'

''Cept if they come outside to walk their dogs, sir, it's an ideal doggy walk.'

'What's that?' Moore snapped.

'It's very secluded with trees along the pavement on both sides. Limes, I believe, and flowering cherry. Very pretty in a couple of months' time.'

'Well house-to-house teams can't wait for the bloody trees to blossom, Howard. They're already on their way. Preliminary enquiries.' Moore sounded brisk. 'With the Incident Room jacked up here in the building, you'll know all the chaps.'

'This Bray, sir. I remember, about five years ago, hadn't he bought an old barn of a place?'

'That's right.'

'Insured it for some ridiculous sum, and it burnt down a couple of months later, on Bonfire Night?'

'Same chap.'

'His wife was roasted alive. He married again in less than a year.'

'You sound sceptical, Howard. I remember, too, but nothing was proved.'

'Still open.'

'We're onto something entirely different, Howard.'

'Yes, sir. It's just, with me, the name Bray always rings a bell: Fraud Squad thought they had something on him once.'

'But they didn't.'

'Seemed not, sir.'

'Someone else was sent down. Hope you're not biased, Howard.'

''Course not, sir.'

'Wrong way to start your enquiries.'

'It's just, I was reminded. This body . . . Bray found her.'

'Well, she was his sister-in-law, and in his drive.'

'Of course.' Robeson's priority on any case of murder was to find the motive. 'P'raps it was a freak accident. Who'd want to shoot a harmless woman of twenty-six? What possible motive?'

'Find it, Howard. Unless we have some maniac on the loose.'

'I'll get up to The Firs, sir, and take Sergeant Mills with me.' Robeson respected his boss's methods of working when leading a hunt. There was no better detective at the Divisional Headquarters of the CID than Superintendent John Moore. Robeson shared his enthusiasm, his attention to detail, his insistence that everything reported was cross-checked over and over. And whatever information of slightest importance came in, it was for Robeson to go out and get it again, first-hand.

He said goodbye to the afternoon he had hoped to spend bird-watching on the Dray Estuary, and rang Mills.

A little later, they were on their way from Headquarters to the city outskirts known as the posh part, to visit The Firs.

The big iron gates stood open. The entrance between them was hung with white tape. Robeson parked his car outside and, acknowledging the uniformed officer standing guard, he and Mills ducked in.

Policemen were scouring the driveway and grounds for footprints, tyre marks, spent bullets, forensic evidence, anything. Robeson and Mills trod carefully across the drive, pausing about two yards from the foot of the stone steps leading up to the front door. Although the girl had been blasted from behind with a gun, there was only a six-inch smear of darkening blood to show where she had fallen. Robeson bit his thick lower lip, and a shock of curly brown hair fell across his broad forehead as he shook his head. In spite of his long experience in the Force, he still was not completely hardened to murder. He led the way up the steps, rang the bell, and waited. It seemed a long time before the door edged open a few inches, and a pale face appeared around the gap.

'Good afternoon, ma'am. I'm Detective Chief Inspector Howard Robeson, CID.' He held out his card. 'Mrs Bray?'

Shaking her head, the young woman clung onto the handle of the door with both hands, her face as pale as if she were confronting a ghost. 'I'm Julie.'

'Don't be nervous, luv. I'm extremely sorry to be calling at such a time. But is Mr Bray . . . ?'

He paused. The door edged open a fraction wider. 'If it's possible . . . if he's available . . . ?'

Julie whispered, 'He's in the libr'y. Asleep I 'spect. I mean, I know, I heard 'im snoring. I hadn't better . . .'

'Perhaps Mrs Bray?'

'I'll see. I think the doctor have give 'er something, but . . .' She pushed the door almost closed in their faces and disappeared. She reappeared a few moments later, wiping her thin hands on her flowered overall as if her nerves had made them sweat: 'Mrs Bray, she says it's all right. She's in the drawing room.' Julie led them there and disappeared again.

Helena stirred in her armchair.

'Please don't get up, Mrs Bray,' Robeson said. 'This is Sergeant Mills, my colleague. We are most extremely sorry.'

He had not expected to see anyone so young. Bray the solicitor was heavy-jowled and middle-aged. His wife reminded Robeson of a favourite actress in his youth, a young Shirley MacLaine; she had the same shade of chestnut gold hair, worn short with a fringe glinting like fire. These slanting eyes were brown, but there was the familiar, small tilted nose.

She said, 'Please, do both sit down, won't you?'

'Thank you.' Robeson recognised the calm of someone a doctor had seen fit to sedate, but who was too devastated to give way to sleep. Someone who nevertheless was still in control, capable of giving a clear account. 'We could come back another time, if you'd rather,' he said, to sound sympathetic and understanding. He preferred not to waste time.

'It's quite all right,' she drawled.

'Perhaps if you could give me just a short account of what you did this morning, and your sister – anything unusual.'

'My husband was going to London. On business. I mean my husband. He was going. Going in his car. To London. First thing.' She took a sharp breath. 'But his car . . . it wouldn't . . . it wasn't . . . He had to take it to the garage.' She paused. Talking seemed an effort. 'I said . . . I would cook lunch. I mean, he could go after.' She stopped for breath. 'When he had gone – I mean, to the garage – I made coffee.' She stopped again. 'For me and Annaliese. I made the coffee. About . . . about eleven o'clock I made the coffee. Then . . . then . . . Annaliese went out.' She sank back in her chair.

Robeson thought for a moment that she was going to fall asleep. 'Do you know where she went? Up the road? Down the road?'

'Oh no,' Helena rallied. 'Never out. I mean, not . . . not without me. The, the cars . . . in the road. It's the cars . . . the cars. Without me . . . she couldn't hear the cars.'

Robeson waited a moment. 'Then where?'

'She used to walk . . . around the golf links. From here . . . the path goes . . .'

'How long was she usually gone?'

'I was cooking . . . I was cooking . . .' She passed her hand over her eyes: 'I expected her back . . . p'raps in an hour. About twelve.'

'I presume you were at the back of the house, in the kitchen. Didn't you hear anything? Like a bang, or a shot?'

She shook her head. 'No. I was cooking.'

'Nothing at all?'

'Only the bells . . . I heard the bells. I closed the window. They spoilt it.'

'Spoilt what?'

'They spoilt Mozart.'

'I see. Do you mean the bells from the church up the road? St Mark's, isn't it?'

She nodded. 'I turned it up. My cassette player. And . . . and I shut the window. I . . . I wanted to listen . . . to Mozart.'

'I see. So you heard nothing from outside?'

'I was thinking . . . was thinking . . .' She sounded half asleep.

'Can you remember what you were thinking, luv?' Robeson was apt to call everyone 'luv' when they looked so young and vulnerable, and in her state of mind.

She drawled, 'Of a friend. A friend . . . And lunch. And Annaliese. If she would be in . . . in to lay the table.'

'Then what, luv?'

'I laid it. I laid it myself. The table. I mean the table. Because . . . she didn't come. Anna . . . I mean, Anna . . . liese . . . She didn't come. Laurence didn't come. Nobody . . . nobody came . . .' She gulped air, her shoulders heaved, and she lay back.

'It's all right, luv.' Robeson stood up. 'We won't worry you any more. I'm terribly sorry. Perhaps if you could get a good sleep. Is your doctor coming back?'

Helena recovered herself: 'I'm sorry.' She sat upright again. 'I'm all right. It's just. It's just that then . . . then I went to look. I opened the front door . . .' She jerked in more great gulps of air. 'I opened it . . . just as Laurence's

71

car turned in . . .' She paused as if gathering strength to go on. 'And I wondered why he braked. And got out.' Her voice trailed, caught in a sob. She flopped back again against her cushion. In one explosive rush, she added, 'Then I saw her.'

'We are most deeply sorry. You must try to get some sleep.' He glanced at Mills. 'Before we go, we'd just like to say hallo to Julie, if we may? Perhaps she'll bring you a nice cup of tea.'

They found their own way to the kitchen, admiring as they went, the wide hallway with its highly polished heavy mahogany table, lofty ceiling, and gilt-framed landscape paintings. Robeson tapped lightly on the open kitchen door.

Julie looked up from reading a magazine at the scrubbed deal table. A little boy in blue dungarees sat wide-legged on the red, vinyl-tiled floor, tearing a sheet of paper into little pieces.

'Now don't look so worried, luv,' Robeson said, going in. 'It's a nasty business, I know, but we're only here because we want to help.' He saw her relax. 'Is there anything at all that you can tell us?'

'I only come at two o'clock. Doctor Jones phoned me neighbour. I don't usually come Saturdays. Had to bring me little boy.' She glanced down at the child who was staring up with soulful blue eyes at the two strange men. She explained, 'Mrs Bray, she got no one of 'er own, see. Not even 'er sister now, she . . . Mrs Bray . . . Oh it was terrible till the doctor . . .' Sniffing, Julie fumbled quickly in the pocket of her overall for a handkerchief, blew her nose, and wiped her eyes.

Robeson waited for her to compose herself.

She sniffed again: 'She's not strong, see. She was ever so bad last week, and now this.' She turned her wet eyes to them: 'But what can I do? She won't eat. I made tea. It's still there.'

'I'm sure it must be a comfort for her just to know you are here, luv. The doctor must have thought so, too.'

The boy got up from the floor and climbed onto his mother's lap, looking curiously from her to them, then back at her.

'That's a bonny lad you have. What's your name, chubby cheeks?'

Nervously the boy coiled a white hanky around his little index finger as if it were a piece of string. He looked at Robeson, then buried his face in his mother's neck.

'It's Ben,' Julie answered for him. 'He's upset. He can't understand. He loved Annaliese. I had to tell him she's gone away.' She sniffed again and blew her nose: 'He's got her hanky. He picked it up, and now he won't let it go.'

Ben turned his head slowly and looked the men up and down as if sizing them up, wondering what they threatened.

'It's all right, son, we're not going to hurt you,' Robeson said like a favourite uncle.

'It's hard,' Julie said. 'Annaliese always kept him amused. They played Noughts and Crosses. She was teaching him to read, too.'

The boy buried his face in her neck again, as if knowing he was being discussed. Julie said, 'A is for Apple. The hanky's got an A on it.' She turned the boy's face with her hand to look at her, and coaxed, 'What else does A stand for, Ben?'

He seemed to consider whether he would answer. Then without moving his face he raised his eyes shyly to the men: 'Aaa . . . is for Aaa . . . na . . .' He clenched his little milk teeth together as he finished her name with a triumphant '*leese*'.

'Jolly good, son,' Robeson smiled. 'Going to show us?'

73

Clenching it, Ben thrust his hand behind his back. 'Mine!'

'All right, son, I'm not going to take it away.'

'Mine,' Ben repeated.

Julie said, 'I let him keep it. I thought what's the use, there's no point, it's only a hanky, see.' She cuddled him. 'If I give it to Mrs Bray, see, well, it's only gonna upset her more, innit? Know what I mean?'

Robeson nodded. 'Possibly. When did he pick it up? Today? In the drive?'

'Oh no. Today. Just now. In the garden. As we come in. Up the path at the side, where she walks.' Julie blew her nose, then wiped her eyes with the back of her hand: 'I mean, where she used to.'

'Yes, luv.'

'Mine,' Ben said.

Robeson looked at Mills. Mills shrugged.

'Ditto,' Robeson said. It was unimportant. 'Don't worry, sonny. 'Course it's yours.'

Julie said, 'It's all right for him. Mr Bray, I mean. Men!' she said vehemently, obviously discounting the fact she was in the presence of two.

'How d'you mean, luv?'

'He escapes. Always escapes. Any trouble, see, an' it's off to the whisky bottle. Know what I mean?'

'But you get on well?'

'Oh yes. All right, I suppose. I know 'im, I worked for him an' his first wife, see.'

Ben wriggled and she set him down on the floor to play with his bits of paper. 'When 'e married again, Mrs Bray that's here now, I was in fer Ben. I was glad of a bit extra. An' Mr Bray said odd hours would suit, see.'

'And you're happy?'

'He can be a quick-tempered sod.'

'Mrs Bray? You're obviously fond of Mrs Bray.'

'Different altogether. Real lady. And Ann . . .' She choked on the name and didn't finish it. 'Both real ladies.'

'Mr and Mrs Bray, I expect they get along well?' Robeson threw the remark casually, as if Julie's answer would be of no importance.

'Yes.' She didn't sound too sure. 'But when I come today he was, well, not drunk, but he'd had a few, know what I mean?'

Robeson's small smile was noncommittal. He knew exactly. He said, 'Mrs Bray probably understands his drinking. You say they get on?'

Julie sniffed. She hesitated, appearing not to be quite sure whether she should speak her mind, or say nothing. She said after a moment, 'They did get on all right, I thought. At first. But . . . about this past year . . .' She paused.

Robeson waited. He was well practised in listening, and letting people talk. But he and his sergeant had not been asked to sit down, though there were other chairs.

'They've been 'aving words lately, I know. An' I've seen 'er crying. Walks round the house, 'er face wet.' Julie sniffed again. 'Thinks I won't notice if she don't wipe 'er eyes.'

'Do you know why she was unhappy?'

'Him, for certain. Oh yes, I know he can be a real charmer, when 'e likes.'

'Do you know any reason why he should make her cry?'

'Annaliese, I expect. Well, I know fer cert'n. They got on all right, I think, till Annaliese come.'

Robeson shifted his feet. He glanced at Mills who was watching Ben playing on the floor.

Julie said, 'He used to say horrid things to Mrs Bray, right in front of Annaliese. He'd say, "Why should I have to put up with someone who can't hear a bloody word, or even speak?"'

Robeson looked at Mills. The sergeant's gaze was wandering round the expensively tiled walls, modern fittings and hygienic worktops of simulated marble.

'He didn't like Annaliese. In fact, I think 'e hated her.'

Robeson pondered. 'Do you see much of any of the neighbours around here?'

'Never.'

'Have you seen anything unusual in this area during the past three or four weeks? Any stranger, or anyone in a car, or even on foot?'

Julie shook her head.

'How do you get here? The buses don't come.'

'Got me bike. Little seat on the back for Ben.'

'I see. And you haven't seen any strangers in the vicinity?'

'No. Only the postman, and the milkman. I don't take much notice of men in cars. I know if any pass me, they'd be on their way to play golf.'

'I see. And Mr Bray – are you sure he's asleep?'

'Sleeping it off, all the whisky. I told you. I know 'im of old.'

'Then we'll come back another time. Have a word with him.'

'My gawd!' Julie clapped her hand to her mouth. Her eyes widened as she appealed, 'You won't say nothing I've said, will you?'

Robeson smiled. It was his policy never to answer questions. 'Don't you worry, luv,' he said, shaking his curly brown head and tapping the side of his nose. A half-broken rule, but some reassurance; a bit of softly softly, velvet treatment often paid off.

In her relief, Julie confided, 'Poor Annaliese. Once, I heard 'im say he'd be glad to be shot of 'er!'

Chapter 7

Laurence stirred in his chair. There was something wrong with his head. Above its throbbing, he heard a tapping on the library door, then someone was saying, 'Mr Bray? Mr Bray?' He jerked himself awake. Julie was standing beside him.

'I'd like to get home with Ben before dark, please, Mr Bray, if I can.'

Pulling himself together, he half rose from the chair with the recollection there was something he had to do: 'Yes, yes, yes, of course, my dear. Run along.'

'There are some chops and veg from lunchtime.'

'Don't worry, don't worry, I'll get something out.'

'Mrs Bray had cooked them. They'd easy heat up.'

He winced. God, his head. He remembered he had needed a stiff drink. He had had one after another while waiting desperately to be alone to make a phone call. But bloody police, Helena's doctor, and God knows who else were here, and seemed they would never go.

'I helped Mrs Bray upstairs. She's asleep now.'

'Thank you, thank you. As you see, she's useless in a crisis.' He pressed his hand to his forehead. 'Probably expect me to starve. So come every day, for a while. But now run along quickly.'

He had no intention of going to a restaurant. They never gave you enough. He had to contact Neville quickly. There was no way but to phone; he would not dare be seen going to his flat. Not now, after this.

Outside, policemen were still in the grounds. God knows what they were doing. He imagined ears and eyes everywhere, listening, watching. In spite of being alone in the house – apart from Helena in a drugged sleep – he checked that the library door was firmly closed. He dialled Neville's number, then curled his hand round the mouthpiece as if afraid that someone behind might hear when he spoke, and clap a hand on his shoulder.

Immediately he heard the voice at the other end, he hissed down the line, 'My God! You've made a bloody cock-up!'

'Who's that?'

'You've killed the wrong bloody woman!'

'Who?'

He spoke less quickly: 'You know who I am.'

'Is that you, Laurie?'

'Don't sound so bloody surprised.' The high-pitched voice was irritation enough. 'You bloody shit!'

'Why? What's up? Changed your plans?'

Laurence's voice had risen involuntarily with anger; he lowered it again. 'Why the bloody hurry? I hadn't even gone.'

'I don't understand, Laurie. Why are you here? Why aren't you in London?'

Laurence felt the hairs on his neck bristle. Neville was acting the innocent. 'So you're going to deny it? Now it's gone wrong?'

'I don't know what you're talking about, Laurie.'

'You know all right, you bloody shits! We agreed an accident. Hit-and-run.'

'Sure. All arranged.'

'Then how d'you explain a bloody bullet? To bloody police? The place is bloody swarming.'

'You sound frightened, Laurie. Why else are you whispering and swearing like crazy?'

'We agreed on an accident.'

'Who's killed whom, Laurie? I'm still not with you.'

'I've been conked out all afternoon. Isn't it in tonight's paper? Or on the six o'clock news?'

'I wouldn't be asking, would I, Laurie?'

'And don't keep saying that bloody name.'

'God, you're touchy. Is it code Troy? We know it's next week when you're away.'

'Then *why the bloody hell today?*'

'I don't understand what you're talking about.'

'Stop pretending, damn you. Just make yourselves scarce, you and your bloody Josh. Lie low.'

'Why?'

'Stop playing. Someone could've seen him. D'you expect to get away with it?' Laurence froze at the thought. If they got Josh, he would talk.

'But Josh hasn't killed anyone.'

'Come off it, she's dead!'

'Who?'

'You know, you bloody shits!'

'You said "the wrong woman". We haven't killed anyone.'

'Who did, then? The same anonymous fairies who set off rockets and sparklers on Guy Fawkes night five years ago?'

There was a gasp at the other end. 'God, Laurie. Going back, aren't you?'

'There was going to be a barbecue. Remember? For children. Remember?'

'But you never sent the invitations.'

'Not the point. Fireworks. Paraffin stove. You made short work of the hut.'

'What you wanted, Laurie. A dreadful accident. No one knew quite how.'

'If anyone comes sniffing about this shooting, I'll see to it they bloody well will know how, and who.'

Neville gasped, then retaliated, 'On whose instructions?'

'You were paid.'

'With whose money? Yours.'

'Prove it. Just try to prove it.'

There was a pause. Then, 'You pig, Laurie, you bloody rotten pig!'

'You could never prove it, and you know it.'

A silence followed. Neville, defensive, said, 'Josh hasn't killed anyone, not this time, not yet. His gun's here and so's he, having a shower.'

'I'm talking of this morning.'

'This morning? He was out.'

'Where?'

'Probably looking. Like you said.'

'Nothing was said about a bloody bullet.'

'It wasn't Josh.'

Laurence was incredulous. 'Hasn't he told you?'

'He would. He's a lovely man.'

'I'm not paying for a cock-up.'

'You'll have to. I mean, pay something. His time.'

'You bled me white after the fire.'

'That's history.'

'I was a mug. You had nothing on me. Listen Neville, I'm not monkeying. Code name Troy, it's off. Everything's finished. Understand?'

'You'll have to pay Josh for . . .'

'Don't come near. Never. Ever! Understand?'

'Josh'll want some money.'

'He can whistle.'

'But Laurie, his time cruising to learn her movements when she was housebound, and you never said.'

'I'm not paying for a bloody cock-up.'

'No cash? And you expect Josh to keep quiet?'

'You shits!' Laurence gripped the receiver as if it were a neck he wanted to strangle. 'All right. I'll think. But give me time. In the meantime, keep well away.' He snatched up a cushion to put over the receiver to smother any sound it might make as he replaced it. Hell, what was he thinking? Who was there to hear? And he had the right to phone in his own house.

It was getting dark. He would not switch on a light; he preferred not to attract the attention of the few men still in the garden. Someone might come to the door.

He settled in his big leather armchair, lit a cigar, poured a whisky and gulped it down. Perhaps the hair of the dog. Hit-and-run could be explained and defended. It involved no serious problems for the culprits who were caught. Especially if there were no reliable witnesses. The victim's car had, for no accountable reason 'come right across my path'. Perhaps it had tried to avoid a dog. Sometimes the hit-and-run driver rustled up a tear-jerking variation of speeding to see a sick granny. The result, with luck, a fine, a suspension, or both. At worst, a few months for manslaughter. But a gun . . . !

A gun. Back in his own office at Headquarters, Robeson reflected on his visit to The Firs. He mulled over his brief interview with Mrs Bray; his chat with Julie; the non-appearance of Mr Bray, asleep in his library.

The afternoon hours that Robeson had hoped to spend bird-watching on the Dray Estuary passed unnoticed. His mind concentrated on today's murder; a challenge that raised his adrenalin level to match the ever-rising pile of paperwork on his desk. Copies of statements, lists of exhibits, correspondence with solicitors, and cardboard folders bulging with partially completed court files.

His priority on any case of murder was to find the motive.

Today's killing appeared to have been the result of a maniac with a gun used at random. There seemed to be no possible connection between the murderer and his victim. No motive. But it was early yet.

Tomorrow there would be a systematic search of the road to the golf links. There would be police tape between the lamp posts and trees, and a brush sweep. Policemen in uniform would ask questions in the street. Perhaps in a few days' time forensic investigation, or the ballistic experts, would come up with something to work on from the one bullet so far discovered by the pathologist.

Robeson got up, stretched out his big arms, and pressed back his broad shoulders to loosen up after the hours he had spent at his desk. The daylight had faded. This evening at least he would spend with Janet; it could be his last for a while if this case got moving. Tomorrow there would be a press conference; appeals to the public to notify the police if they had noticed anything suspicious during the past few days, or seen any strangers in the area. And the house-to-house teams would be handing in their questionnaires, and there would be statements to study.

It occurred to Robeson, even without the reports yet from the experts, that the fatal shot might have been fired from a close-range weapon, probably a revolver. And it might not have been aimed from the open entrance to the drive as it had seemed at first. Quite possibly it had come from the direction of the golf links, through a gap between the trees. In which case it was the mindless act of a madman without motive.

Or deliberate murder. By someone who had a grudge against the Brays.

He reached for his tweed jacket, hung over the back of his chair. He had a long memory, and access to files on past cases, but he could think of nothing that had any connection with Bray's young sister-in-law. Who could possibly have had a grudge against a seemingly innocent woman with a speech and hearing handicap? It did not add up.

He ran his fingers through his hair. It had been a longer day than he had anticipated. Tomorrow he would see the secretary or steward of the Golf Club, get a list of members and their home addresses, and find out which of them had been playing on Saturday, 23rd March. He would also need the names and home addresses of any visitors who had played or had a drink in the bar; in fact, details of anyone at all who might have been seen on the fairway.

He made his way through the outer offices, along the corridor and down to the car park. Before he slipped behind the wheel of his car, he glanced back at Head-quarters. In his opinion it was a concrete monstrosity banded with glass, but it was geared to cope with modern crime. And he found an immense satisfaction in his work, even if 'enjoyment' was not the right word to describe what some of it involved.

Driving home, he pondered on how many late nights might lie ahead. How many of Janet's good meals would spoil, drying up in the oven waiting for him to come home? He smiled to himself. In another month's time, he would not mind so much getting up in the early mornings; he would hear the dawn chorus of the blackbirds and song thrushes. But he hoped the bugger who had committed this senseless, wicked crime would be caught long before then.

Chapter 8

Robeson was impatient for action. Public response to police appeals for help was slow. Hardly surprising since The Firs, where the shooting took place, was situated at the far end of Links Road. Few people passed there unless on their way to play golf. And detached houses in the vicinity, hidden in their own grounds by trees, were occupied by the kind of people who minded their own business.

He glanced round the Incident Room. His dark eyes rested on Detective Sergeant Mills poring over some of the statements already returned by a house-to-house team.

'Anything to bite on yet, Roger?'

'Not much, sir. Two DCs have been at the Golf Club all morning. Like you briefed.'

'Aye. Should get some light. We'll quiz every member, either at the links, or their HAs. What else?'

'About fifty calls.'

'That all?'

'Some from nutters.'

'Skip them for now. Anything useful?'

'One chap'd noticed a car – the same car – several times lately, driving slowly in Links Road.'

'What time of day?'

'Seems it was morning sometimes, but a couple of after-noons, too.'

'Where exactly? Anywhere near The Firs?'

'No. Well, yes. I mean Links Road. He couldn't say specifically what part. Sort of up and down.'

'Well, what was he doing there himself?'

'Delivering from a mail van. Sounds like parcels.'

'Did he describe the car?'

'It was green. He thinks. Perhaps a Mondeo.'

'Dark green? Light green?'

'Just "green" I've got down here.'

Robeson stiffened his thick lips. That was unlike Mills; there were shades of green. He controlled his irritation. 'Well, what sort of condition?'

'Nothing outstanding apparently.'

'And the driver?'

'I asked, sir. The informant said he wasn't thinking at the time to notice. Just remembers the car.'

'Bloody useless. A car going slow down Links Road. Most do. It's on the way to nowhere unless you live there, or play golf.'

'Or deliver things,' Mills finished. He grinned. 'I suppose it depends on what you call slow, sir. Thirty? Or a crawl, as in kerb?'

Robeson grunted. In spite of being annoyed about not having the exact colour of the car, he liked Mills and his repartee – it showed a lively spirit that kept one sane in the darker moments of the job: 'Well, which was it?'

'I didn't get the chance to ask, sir. The informant rang off without giving his name.'

Robeson clamped his mouth shut. He was getting nowhere. He had formed no picture in his mind yet as to a possible motive for the killing, and wondered if there was one. It seemed possible there was a maniac at large with a gun, taking pot shots at innocent people for the hell of it. 'Well, it shouldn't be difficult to trace a postman if we want to know more. And we shall.'

He stood, leaning against a table. The room buzzed.

There was plenty of enthusiasm, a murder meant interest as well as overtime.

Some detectives, in turn, read part of their statements aloud. They had all been recorded and cross-referenced. Phones rang, ideas flowed, officers studied statements and questionnaires.

Robeson knew all about paperwork. It was the story of every copper's life, and of his own, except when something of this magnitude came up. Now geared to action, he wanted to crack this case quickly. And so far, dammit, he hadn't a clue. Not a single lead.

Mills looked up from his desk. 'There's a report here, sir; a woman saw lots of cars in Links Road last Saturday by the church. Seems there was a wedding.'

'What time?'

'Around midday. Perhaps later, she wasn't sure. She was walking her dog.'

'Well, that's easily checked. Whose wedding? We'll get a guest list. Names of everyone who attended the service.' He pushed a lock of curly brown hair back from his forehead; he would really have to get it cut when he could make time. He suggested, 'Perhaps someone waiting outside the church may have seen something, or someone they weren't expecting to see. Scout around.'

'Yes, sir. But there's more here. Later, the same informant noticed a car in Links Road; it almost stopped outside The Firs, then went on quite quickly.

'Which way? To the golf links?'

'No sir. It had come from there. Or it may have just turned. Apparently some cars make a U-turn at the entrance to the links.'

'What time was this?'

'She wasn't sure. About a quarter to one, as far as she can remember. She'd been waiting down by the church, hoping to see the bride and groom.'

'And did she?'

'Apparently not. She gave up waiting, and walked home with her dog.'

'Where does she live, then?'

Mills flicked back the page. 'At Pine Ridge, Links Road. PC Walsh has scribbled beside the address that it's almost opposite The Firs.'

'A green car, did you say?'

'No, sir. That was the postman who phoned in. This lady was quizzed by PC Walsh and Smith, house-to-house.'

'What colour was it, then?'

'Cream, she thought.'

'And who exactly is this informant?'

'A Lady Glen-Esk.' Mills looked up from the notes he was referring to, and grinned. ' "Glen-Esk with a hyphen, please", PC Walsh has written.'

'Any more?' Robeson grunted.

Mills glanced back at his notes: 'The driver wasn't a stranger. She knew his face, but couldn't put a name to it.'

'Then who was he?' Robeson stood up to his full six-foot-two. 'It's crucial. That was around the time Mr Bray arrived home and discovered his sister-in-law's body lying in the drive.'

'She said she couldn't think of his name.'

'And didn't Walsh press?'

Mills shrugged. 'She apparently altered that statement to, "I don't know his name; I only know him by sight." '

Robeson insisted, 'But she admits she did recognise him? At least the face was familiar.'

'Yes sir.'

'Did she describe what he looks like?'

'She was asked to, but she wasn't very forthcoming. She said her eyes aren't as good as they were.'

'But they were good enough to recognise a man driver in a cream car,' Robeson had met these sort of people before;

they would give a mite of information, then back off if they thought they were getting too involved.

Mills read from the page in front of him, 'He may have a moustache. Or a beard.' He paused, and with a wry grin he glanced up at Robeson and added, 'or . . . he may not.'

'Nothing to bloody smile about.'

'No, sir.'

'Sounds a bloody good witness. The sort we can do without. She'll have to do better. She must be pressed.'

'By comments on the form, sir, it would seem that Lady Glen-Esk, with a hyphen please, is not the sort of person who likes to be pressed.'

'Then she'll have to bloody well lump it. I want to know who she saw, even if only to eliminate him.'

'Yes, sir.'

'If that person is in the clear, at around that vital time, he may have seen something, or someone, else. Even if she didn't.'

It was the only information Robeson had had so far that might just offer a possible lead. He was not going to let it pass. Glen-Esk with a bloody hyphen indeed. Perhaps if he paid deference to her hyphenated aristocracy, and turned on the charm that Janet said he had plenty of when he wanted something, he could sharpen Her Ladyship's memory. He would let her know he was coming to see her, to have a word.

'Fancy a nice walk around the golf links, Roger?' He saw Mills glance towards the window, rain just starting to hit the glass: 'On second thoughts, you've plenty on your plate.' He scanned the room over the heads of officers bent over their desks. Perhaps one of Lady Glen-Esk's own sex would be a better choice. Whether it would or not, he could do with the assistance of someone as efficient as Detective Inspector Mary Starks. Beneath the stylish cut of her fair hair was a shrewd brain that had proved itself before and earned her promotion. He caught her eye and called her over.

Pine Ridge was screened by trees. The wide wooden gate, in need of paint, was off its hinges. Permanently open, it had settled into the ground. Weeds punctuated the gravel drive.

Using his size 11 clad feet, Robeson cleared a pile of dead leaves against the porch door that was contrarily fitted to open outwards. Inside, more leaves were stuck like postage stamps on the dark-tiled floor. He noted the mildew, a broken cane chair, and the flaking, scuffed front door; a stark contrast to The Firs, the elegantly kept house of the same age on the opposite side of the road.

He rang the bell. A dog yapped, and after several moments the door opened a few inches. Thin fingers unfastened a series of safety chains: 'Lady Glen-Esk?' Robeson asked with a smile, and showed his card. 'Detective Chief Inspector Robeson. This is my colleague, Inspector Mary Starks.'

Her ladyship clutched a Pekinese under her arm. In spite of her permed white head reminiscent of a dandelion clock, and her lined face, she looked, with her tiny waist and long fluted skirt, as delicate as a Coalport figurine.

They followed her into the drawing room and accepted her invitation to sit down. The chintz-covered armchairs had seen better days. Robeson felt a spring give beneath his weight.

She wasted no time. 'I understand you'd like to know more about the car I saw on Saturday.'

Robeson liked the gentle voice. 'We would, and do, appreciate your help.'

'Well, I really told them all I know. They called, you know. Two very young policemen. In uniform. Not like you.'

Robeson was not sure if that was a reflection on his being in his late forties, or the fact that he was wearing civvies. Perhaps it was that his mop of brown hair was showing grey in front of his ears. 'We do appreciate the help you gave them. But we wondered, can you possibly recall a little more? The driver's name, for instance?'

'I am so sorry. I really can't. When you get to my age . . . But I know I've seen him before somewhere.'

'Just once?'

'On no. I wouldn't remember just once.' She put the dog down on the worn carpet. It turned its short wrinkled muzzle towards Robeson, glared, then waddled from the room: 'I suppose I must have seen him . . . perhaps several times. I don't know. I can't think where.'

'It would be a great help if you could remember perhaps just a little more.' Robeson chose his words carefully and spoke gently. He recognised the good manners of someone who had seen better days.

'Oh, I have been trying to think, since you rang. But when you get to my age . . .'

Robeson smiled. He had plenty of time if there was the slightest hope. He changed his tack. 'It's a nice little dog you have.'

'Henry? A darling, isn't he? He's such company. And a good little watch dog.'

'You live alone?'

'Oh yes, this past twenty years. We came back to England when my husband retired.' She shook her head, pursing her lips. 'But the climate killed him.'

The dog waddled back and she took it onto her lap: 'It was this climate, I'm sure. So damp, after Africa.'

Robeson nodded sympathy. Perhaps Africa explained her

90

skin; it was like off-white crepe paper. Though it was easy to picture her in some British colony, well protected under a sunshade. He could see her pink scalp through the thin white hair. 'But you've not thought of moving?'

'I'm all right. Since the Poll Tax. I'm all right with the Council Tax or whatever tax they call it now,' she said, ignoring the question.

He glanced at the Adam-style fireplace; the coal burning in its iron grate was scarcely enough to reflect in the brass fender. Perhaps any saving on household rates would enable her to stay here. He remarked, 'It's a lovely big house.'

'Oh yes, yes. But too big. Impossible to keep on a fixed income.' She glanced up at the wall.

He followed her eyes to the large sepia photographs in old-fashioned frames that he supposed were her chronicled past: 'Do you know your neighbours, Mr and Mrs Bray, at The Firs, on the other side?'

'Only on nodding terms. With him I mean, but Mrs Bray . . .'

'Did you know her sister?'

'Oh yes, such a sweet girl.' She paused to stroke Henry, and nuzzle him up to her to kiss him on the top of his head.

Robeson glanced at Mary. She was too clever to produce her notebook unless strictly necessary. She would know Lady Glen-Esk must talk, and nothing was more off-putting than seeing one's every word being written down.

'I met them sometimes, out walking. But she couldn't very well – the sister, I mean. Something wrong with her foot.' Her hand stroked Henry's silky head, and his eyes closed in ecstasy. 'And it was so sad, you know. Did you know she was stone deaf?' Robeson nodded. 'But she always smiled and made such a fuss of Henry.'

'Did you ever see them with anyone else, or notice any stranger, or any other car?'

91

'I can't really think ... when you get to my age.' She looked lost for a moment. 'But...' She stopped short. 'Something nearly came just now when we mentioned the house.'

'Then perhaps if we recap.'

'Oh no, it's completely gone. Oh bother, bother.'

Robeson waited. If he smiled and looked as if he understood, perhaps she would relax and remember.

She said, 'Sometimes I can't recall what happened yesterday. And yet, things years ago are vivid. It's like that when you get to my age.'

'Was it something to do with the house?'

'I think it might have been.' She paused to reflect. 'No, it won't come. Oh, bother.' She paused, then brightened. 'But I do recall something. Something else. But no, it wouldn't be important.'

'Anything may be important. Try to remember.'

She made the dog settle on the sofa beside her. 'Well, let me see, what day is it today?'

'Monday.'

'Ah yes, of course. Well on Saturday I was walking with Henry, and I remember now ... yes ... Mr Bray passed me in his car on the way home.'

'What time was that?'

'Oh, I really can't say, not exactly. Perhaps a quarter to one.'

'What sort of car does he drive?'

'A big brown one. It's a Rover. I know that, a friend of mine has one just like it.'

'Did Mr Bray see you?'

'Oh yes, he raised his hand and smiled.'

'You're quite sure?'

'Oh yes.'

'But you did say you can't see too well.'

'Officer, I can assure you it was Mr Bray. I know him well by sight.'

'Like you know the other gentleman, whose name you can't recall?'

'Oh much better of course, living so near.'

Robeson studied her. Tucked into the tiny waistband of her fluted black skirt, she was wearing a mauve silk blouse fastened to the neck with matching pearl buttons, and embellished with a large diamanté brooch. He said, 'Did you see Mr Bray in his brown car before, or after, you saw a man in a cream car stop outside The Firs?'

'Oh, he didn't stop, or only nearly. He drove on.'

'You mean the cream car?'

'Yes.'

'Well, was that before or after you saw Mr Bray?'

She looked into her lap.

Robeson guessed Mary was noting every pause, every twitch of the pale lips, as Lady Glen-Esk thought back.

She looked up. 'Of course. I must have seen Mr Bray first. He passed me when I was down the road, walking home.'

'How far down? How long did it take you to get up here?'

'Oh, let me see . . . Henry's little legs . . . and he's nearly ten, you know, aren't you, precious?' She smoothed his head: 'I'd say, possibly five minutes.'

'And when you got here, you saw a cream car come from the direction of the golf links, nearly stop outside The Firs, but then drive on.'

'That's right.'

'So it is feasible that Mr Bray had driven into his drive. His car may have been parked inside, where it could be seen from the gates.'

'Oh yes, officer. That seems very likely.'

'Lady Glen-Esk, you really have been most helpful.' He

glanced at Mary, elegantly informal, her white blouse in contrast to her navy gaberdine raincoat. 'Inspector, is there anything you would like to ask Lady Glen-Esk?'

Mary beamed. Throughout the interview she had been exchanging quiet smiles and sympathetic nods with Her Ladyship: 'Yes I would, please; just one or two things.' Her tone promised a gentle approach. She fixed her full smile and steady brown eyes on the woman stroking her Pekinese: 'Lady Glen-Esk, at one point just now you seemed to remember something. I mean something that for a second reminded you of who it was you saw in the cream car?'

The woman appeared to give the remark her earnest attention, but continued to stroke the dog from obvious habit, the skin of her hand taut and transparent, her fingers banded with rings that could have come straight from Garrard, the Crown Jewellers. She glanced up at the wall, a faraway look in her pale eyes.

Mary noted they were fixed on the picture of a man in a pith helmet, and a young woman in a long dress, her face half hidden by a veiled hat. Around them were natives, naked but for bangles and beads. She prompted, 'Was it the house being too large, or Africa?'

'Oh,' Lady Glen-Esk seemed to wake up. 'I think yes.'

Mary repeated, 'The house, or Africa? I mean, which was it?'

'Oh I loved Kenya.' Lady Glen-Esk seemed to go into a trance, as though recalling better times: 'The people, they were so courteous ... the Bantu tribe, the Kikuyu.' She paused, tightened her lips, and came back to the present. 'But things were changing, even then. My husband always said, when the time came that we had to carry a gun to protect ourselves, we'd emigrate.'

'And that's why you came back?'

'Oh no. He reached retirement. He was editor of an

English-language daily.' She paused. 'Mind you, emigration is probably difficult today with the Rand low and still dropping.' She glanced at a copy of *Cry The Beloved Country* on a small table beside the sofa. 'Poor Africa.'

Robeson did not want to stay too long with nostalgia. He could not imagine Lady Glen-Esk strong enough to hold a gun, let alone fire one. He caught Mary's eye, and with a slight movement of his head egged her to carry on as she had been doing.

Mary said, 'Lady Glen-Esk, a few minutes ago, from what you told us, it seemed your fleeting recollection of who you saw outside The Firs came to you when we were discussing the size of this house.' She paused for that fact to sink in. 'Then you digressed; you told us Mr Bray had passed you in *his* car. Could we get back to what we were talking about before then?'

Lady Glen-Esk looked blank.

'Perhaps if I remind you; you had said that sometimes you can't remember what happened yesterday, but things years ago are vivid.' Mary paused again before going on, 'You then added that just now, something nearly came to you when we mentioned the house.'

The woman was thinking.

Robeson glanced round. The room offered no rival to illustrations in *Good Housekeeping*, but it had interesting relics: maps, a globe, a bookcase that overflowed, and quality newspapers.

Mary repeated, 'When we mentioned the house, before that, you had said its upkeep is impossible on a fixed income. Does that help?'

The woman came to life. 'Oh yes, yes, my dear. You are right. I remember.'

Robeson's spirits rose.

Lady Glen-Esk set the dog aside again and clasped her

95

thin hands together. 'I was so interested. So interested when I heard him, I got carried away. But I do love to reminisce, and I so rarely get the chance.'

Robeson could not see the connection.

Mary waited.

Lady Glen-Esk went on, 'Of course it's so sad, these days. But he explained why he had to go back.'

'Who is he?' Mary asked gently. 'And going back where?'

'Such a nice man he was. A little older than you, perhaps, or about your age,' she said looking at Robeson. 'He farms, he told me. The Natal or somewhere.'

Robeson bit his lip. Damn. Was she wandering? Wasting their time after all? He admired Mary's manner as she went on regardless.

'And where did you meet this nice man?'

'Oh, in the town, didn't I say? I'm sorry. I went on the bus. The house was getting on top of me.' She rubbed her hands together.

Robeson mused that the high-ceilinged room could certainly have done with more warmth.

Mary said, 'And you met this man?'

'Yes.'

'Where exactly did you meet him?'

'Oh, in the shop of course. I was determined to go in. I'd really made up my mind.'

'And you met this nice man? Was he a customer? An assistant?'

'Oh no, no, I don't think he was either. I had to wait, you see. And I overheard him talking to a lady at a desk, about Africa, and the troubles. And I simply couldn't resist joining in.'

'And was this the man you had seen in the cream car?'

'Oh no, no. This man was here on holiday, from Africa. I took it his people live here. After I'd joined in their conversation, I remember, the lady said, "This is my brother."'

'Then you still can't place the man you had seen at the wheel of that cream car?'

'Oh yes, yes, I can. Of course, it's clear now.'

Robeson sat up straight.

Mary leaned forward, elbows on her knees, her chin cupped in her hands.

Lady Glen-Esk explained, 'I wanted someone's opinion about the house, whether to sell. It's been such a struggle, a real burden.' She paused. 'I had to wait, he had someone with him. But I saw him as soon as he was free.'

'Can you describe him?'

'Oh dear, I'm not much good ... But I know his name now, of course.' Her pale eyes lit up. 'The man I saw in the cream car was the estate agent, Mr Price.'

Chapter 9

Lady Glen-Esk's porch had let in the rain. Soggy leaves stuck to the detectives' shoes as they made their way out through to the car.

'Not the day for a stroll round the links,' Robeson said, stamping his feet clean before getting in. Nevertheless, with Inspector Starks beside him, he switched the engine on, nosed from the drive, and turned in that direction.

'Keep your eyes open, Mary. For anything. Anything at all. He often used her Christian name when they were working alone. 'I'm going to crawl. As in kerb, Sergeant Mills would say.'

The windscreen wipers swished a clear half-moon, but she wound down her window. Immediately to their left were some ornamental iron gates, and on one of the brick supporting pillars was a nameplate, The Firs. Continuing from the pillar was a brick wall overhung by trees. Some yards further on, almost hidden by branches, was a wooden gate.

Mary read, 'Tradesmen'.

Robeson stopped, and switched the engine off. The whirring wipers gave way to the sound of rain drumming on the roof. 'Tradesmen? The butcher and baker? I thought those days were over.'

'They are, sir, for ordinary mortals. You lug it all home in plastic bags.'

Robeson peered across through her window, since he could not see properly out of the front. 'That's probably been there for years.'

'Looks freshly painted to me, sir.'

'Well, black to match the main entrance.'

'I mean the white sign, sir. Tradesmen.'

He leaned across her to look closer. 'Mmm. Bold enough. Wishful thinking maybe.' He gave a short laugh. 'Well that fits. Typical.'

'Pretentious is she, Mrs Bray?'

'Oh no, no. I wouldn't think so; though I've only met her once, so far. On Saturday, when she was in shock.' He flattened back his damp hair. He had a long memory, and the name Laurence Bray ... But he only said, 'It's her husband. I wouldn't trust him further than his front garden.'

Robeson did finger exercises on the steering wheel. They could see nothing more from here, and he had examined the grounds from the other side of that gate thoroughly over the weekend. Luckily he had caught the weather right, it had been dry. 'The path in there runs for several yards,' he explained so that Mary could share the picture. 'Then on the left, it leads to the back of the house.' He switched on the engine again. 'But if you turn right, it'll take you on around the golf course.'

He slipped into gear and moved off slowly. Within a few yards, before the entrance to the golf links, the road was shaped like a keyhole where cars could turn. He drove straight on and up the slight hill towards the clubhouse at the top. There were only four or five cars parked outside. He passed them and went on a bit further, then turned the car round to face the way they had come. He stopped where thick pines kept off the rain.

The greens were deserted. Down the fairway, between the treetops was the glimpse of a chimney, and an aerial, and the red roof of The Firs. Robeson glanced across at the woods bordering the far side: 'Anyone can walk around over there. In fact, further on there are blackberry bushes. I know people who come picking them, every August and September.' His fingers tapped the steering wheel as he contemplated the easy access. 'No one stops them unless they cause a nuisance, or bring dogs not on a lead.'

Mary said, 'There were probably several people walking on Saturday, it was a lovely day.'

'Don't I know it. I was going to go down to Draymouth.' He reflected on the grey plovers and redshanks he had probably missed; the oystercatchers on the sands, or running along the mud flats, stopping occasionally to prise open a cockle. 'I'd looked forward all the week to a few hours on the estuary, then some bloody wicked beast with no soul had to . . .'

His lips stiffened. He had once thought everyone had a soul. Reluctantly his opinion was changing, in spite of his constant battle with himself not to grow bitter. Murderers had no soul. No bloody soul. They couldn't have a soul. Unless there were grades of soul. Unless souls came in definitive qualities like cuts of meat: Best End, Top, and Prime. With Scrag End for murderers.

He said, 'This Mr Price, I know he plays golf. Mills checked up only recently when Price lost his wife.'

'Seems incredible he'd be involved' Mary said.

'Agreed. You know him?'

'Not personally. But . . .' She pulled a face to express her incredulity. 'Price the estate agent seems the last person on earth.'

'He'll have some perfectly good explanation for being near The Firs at the time that her ladyship says she saw him.' Robeson stroked his chin. 'Probably paused on his way home. May have been lighting a fag.'

'Or he may have been interested,' Mary suggested, 'after

Lady Glen-Esk had asked him about her property. Just looking. Comparing.'

'Quite possible. But he may be able to help us. He could well have seen someone; it was around that very time.' Robeson pushed back a spring of damp hair from his forehead. 'The doctor said the girl had been dead about an hour when he saw her. The time and cause were confirmed at the PM.' He waggled the gear lever to check neutral, then released the handbrake and let the car move silently down the slope towards the clubhouse. Stopping, he said, 'We'll go in and see the steward. I'm sure we'll be allowed to whet our whistle.'

The clubhouse struck warm after the damp outside. But there was nothing ostentatious about it; the small mahogany tables and chairs, and a plain counter bar looked no more than functional.

The steward behind the bar was young. His straight yellow hair, black at the roots, flopped over one eye. He grinned when Robeson flashed his card. 'Your chaps were here for ages, guv. Not been gone long.'

'Well, lucky for you, young man. Sell a few jars, did you? You don't look rushed off your feet.'

'Nah. In uniform? Nothing doing. I shut them in with Tom.'

'The secretary?'

'In the other room, guv. Wanna see 'im?'

'We'll make do with you, young man, for the moment. What about a drink for us then?'

'Nah. Members only.' The boy grinned wickedly. 'What's it going to be?'

Robeson rarely drank on duty, and only ever in half pints; any more, then it was lemonade. But he hoped to learn something, and the weather had fortuitously imposed a little privacy at the right time and place important to his enquiries. The mere handful of members present looked

101

bored. Smoking their pipes and cigarettes near the windows, they gazed out disconsolately at the rain clouds that canopied the sopping green. He could talk to them later if need be. He ordered his half pint, and a shandy for Mary, automatically sliding his money over when the brimming glasses were pushed dribbling towards them. Avoiding getting his sleeves wet, he leaned on the counter while Mary perched herself on a high stool.

Within minutes, they were discussing the purpose of his visit. Yes, the boy had often seen the two young women out walking around the course. And yes, just sometimes he had seen the slightly lame one on her own.

Robeson said, 'Tom, the secretary, has he given my men a list of members and their HAs – I mean their home addresses?'

'Well . . . if that's what they came for, yes, for certain, guv, but I can still ask. Wanna see him?'

'Not for a moment. You'll do.' Robeson sipped his beer, then set down the glass: 'Can you tell me: were there many playing on Saturday?'

'Ooo . . .' The boy scratched his eyebrow, its blackness a stark contrast to his yellow hair. 'Quite a few. I think. Well, I know there were, actually, we sorted 'em through, me and Tom, with your chaps.' He tossed his head.

Robeson mused that Janet would describe his hair as straight as a yard of pump water. But then, she said rude things about his own; it was like corkscrews grown wonky, especially when it got wet. He said, 'Good, it'll be helpful to have the names.' He did not want to single out anyone in particular, but he was impatient to verify that Mr Price's name was among them. 'I suppose you know all the members pretty well?'

'Oh yes. Well, most. You get to, listening here. If they don't drink, they pass through.'

'Friendly, are they?'

'Mostly. One or two snobs. Don't bother me.'

'And you, yourself, were you here on Saturday?'

'Yes.'

'What time d'you come?'

'Here by ten. Like always.'

'How d'you come? D'you drive?'

'Sure. My banger's out there.'

'Can you remember seeing anyone as you came on Saturday? In Links Road, or near the course? Anyone you don't usually see?'

The boy shook his head, hair flopping over one eye. 'Nah. Can't say I did. I'm never much in Links Road.'

'Anything. A car . . . anyone behaving suspiciously?'

'Nope. Didn't see nothing like that.'

'Have you heard if anyone else saw anything?'

'Nope. A bloody mystery if you'll pardon my French. Makes you think, someone out there shooting willy-nilly. Could've been me, you, anybody.'

'Or you, Mary.' Robeson glanced at her perched so quietly, contemplating her shandy. He guessed she was not thinking of anything but the job, but he liked to draw her in, let no one mistake her for a puppet.

She agreed, 'It doesn't bear thinking about. Who's safe until he's caught?'

Robeson looked at the boy again, and jerked his head back. 'These chappies behind me?'

'They've been done, guv, like me and Tom. The policemen took statements.'

'Good.' Robeson wondered how to winkle the information he wanted. He would get it when he got back to the Incident Room, but he wanted it now. He took a leisurely swig at the beer; he didn't like it much. Unhurriedly he put down the glass and glanced round the room, and towards the wet windows. 'What a difference in the weather. It was lovely on Saturday.'

The boy mopped the counter with a small towel: 'Not bad yesterday, either. Well, least dry.' Robeson did not want to waste time on the weather; he knew it was changeable. He had been grateful for the dry weekend, but he said: 'Makes all the difference, doesn't it, the weather. Did many play yesterday?'

'My day off.'

'Oh.' Robeson was not getting far. He supposed he would have to wait until he got back to study the statements. He resumed his matter-of-fact style. 'I suppose weekends, Saturdays and Sundays, are best for businessmen?'

The boy pushed his towel aside. He picked up a glass tankard, scrutinising it against the light. 'That's right. Get the real toffs in the week.'

'Who d'you call the real toffs?'

'Well . . . you know,' he said, picking up a clean linen cloth to polish the glass. 'You know. With the money.'

Robeson took a long drink, put down his glass, and wiped his mouth. 'Well, businessmen and professional men, plenty of them have got money.'

The boy grinned: 'Well, yes, but they're usually too busy making it in the week.' He hung up the tankard. 'It's then the toffs come in their big cars. Retired wallahs, or those that can afford to skive off. Know what I mean?'

Robeson returned the grin: 'Yeah.' He paused, then spoke as if he had had an afterthought that was unimportant. 'I can think of one businessman in the city, said to be worth a bit.' He paused again, then spoke in measured tones as if what he was going to say had only just occurred to him. 'He's a golfer. Perhaps you may know him. Mr Price? The estate agent?'

'Oh sure, nice chap. Big fella, lovely looker, with sideburns.'

Robeson showed little interest beyond agreeing. He smiled at Mary. 'It suits you, doesn't it, Mary? Sitting there

104

on that stool, swigging shandy.' She returned his smile; she had worked with him often enough to sense his ploys. He looked back at the boy and resumed the conversation as if it were of no particular consequence: 'He played on Saturday, didn't he . . . er . . . Mr Price?'

'Did he?' The boy tossed his hair from his eye. 'Let me think. Nah. Actually I don't think he did.'

'I mean Saturday morning,' Robeson clarified. 'Perhaps till lunchtime?'

'Nah. I don't think so. Not this Saturday just gone.'

'Really?' Robeson feigned mild surprise, as if whether Mr Price played or not didn't in the least matter: 'I know Mr Price quite well,' he lied. 'I had an idea he was going to play. Perhaps he just came in for a drink?'

The boy found another glass to inspect but pushed it aside, seemingly content to idle. 'Nah. I don't think so. Well I don't remember seeing him, not at all on Saturday.' He paused, reflecting. 'It was a nice day, but I don't think he played – I'd have seen him. I was here until two o'clock.'

Robeson shrugged.

The boy flicked his hair. 'On the other hand, I suppose somehow I could have missed him.'

'Oh, it's not important.'

'But I can't think how.'

Robeson cut in, 'He was probably busy and changed his mind.' He glanced at Mary who, reading his mind, finished her drink.

He turned back to the boy, and drawled, 'It's quite a restful haven you have here. Wish we could stay. But still, we've had a nice little ride around in spite of the weather.' He nodded a cheerful, 'And thanks for your help.'

Mary took her cue, smiled her thanks across the counter, and got down from the stool.

*

105

Driving back to Headquarters, Robeson asked, 'What have you gleaned this morning, Mary?'

'Not much, sir. I think Lady Glen-Esk did see Price. And that young steward could have missed seeing him.'

'So it's back to nit-picking through all the statements. D'you realise, Mary, we're only as good as our informants? We need tip-offs.'

'We'll get them, sir.'

'Ever the optimist.'

'Price may have seen someone.'

'Yes. That's very likely. I'll have a word. He would probably rather come in than have me calling at his office.'

At that moment, Ian Price sat slumped over his office desk. The scent of glasshouse pink carnations, and the fresh bowl of deep red, double camellias, should have lifted his spirits. Instead, they deepened his black mood; they were too much like a sequel to what had happened last night when he arrived home. At the top of the steps, by the front door, he had found Miss Roberts.

'Whatever are you doing here, Gail?'

'Saw the light,' she had giggled. 'Thought . . . thought I'd like to see you.'

'At this hour?' It was chilly, and he had scanned the small figure hugging herself with her arms; the red mohair coat, the face partly shadowed beneath the coach lamp on the wall. 'My dear Gail, it's cold. I do believe you're shivering. I'll run you home. Come along.' He had moved towards the steps.

She had stayed, her back to the door. 'Don't want to go. Want to talk.'

'But it's late. And you shouldn't be here.'

'Why not? I want to stay with you. Alone with you.'

'Don't be silly, Gail.'

'Alone. For once.'

'Now come along. Like a good girl.'

'Mmm,' she purred. 'You say that . . . so nice. You make me fe . . .'

'Come along now,' he had interrupted firmly. 'You can tell me whatever it is you want to tell me, tomorrow. In the office.'

She had not moved.

He had put his hand on the shoulder of her rough, hairy coat: 'Have you left your mother in the house alone?'

'She isn't a child.'

'No, but whatever would she think?'

'You must be very lonely now.'

'She'd worry to know you were out, Gail.'

Angrily she had raised her voice: 'I'm not a child either, I'm a woman!' She had pressed against him: 'I'm a woman.' She had started to rave. 'Don't you understand? I'm a woman!'

He had pushed her aside, felt for his door key, switched on the hall light and hustled her in to sort this out. The bungalow was fairly isolated, but there were night owls who walked their dogs in the lane; if anyone heard her shouting they would have come to see what was happening.

Inside, she had become quiet at once. He had faced the triumph in her eyes. 'Well, Gail, what're you thinking of? This won't do.'

The living room light was harsh. She had ringed her eyes with eyeliner, and the blusher on her high cheekbones clashed with her red coat. She had smiled. 'Where are the cats?'

'I asked you Gail, what's the big idea?'

'Where are the cats?' she had repeated sweetly, looking round,

'You didn't come here to see the cats at this unearthly hour.'

107

'Well, tell me, where are they?'

'Asleep in bed and that's where we should be,' he had snapped and immediately rectified his mistake. 'I'm taking you home, Gail. And for God's sake don't make another scene outside,' He had not liked her smile. She had clutched her hairy red coat around herself with her hands deep in its pockets. 'We'll have to talk about this tomorrow, Gail. When we've both had time to think, and be sensible. Now come along.'

He had thought by her slight movement that she had agreed. She had removed her hands from her pockets. But before he knew it, she had slipped out of her coat and thrown it across the table. 'My God!' He had blinked in disbelief, confronted by her nakedness from the waist up; small, pointed breasts, nipples erect, areolas decorated with scarlet lipstick. 'Good grief, woman!' He had snatched up the coat and thrown it at her. 'Cover yourself up! My God, what're you thinking of?'

She had held her coat but did not move.

He had read the invitation in the narrowed eyes. She wanted him to attempt to assist, forcing him to touch her. He had stepped back: 'Go on. Quickly. Put it on!'

Her lips had quivered.

He knew he should feel sorry for her. He had spoken as kindly as he dared. 'Hurry up.' How often in the last few years he had longed for a woman; how often his groin had ached from the celibacy inflicted on him by Carol's neuroses. 'Do as I say, Gail.'

She had recovered herself. Their eyes met, hers brazen.

He had glanced away. Perhaps if she had used a little more subtlety he might ... Oh, God, would he? He still could. Throw her on the bed in the adjoining room. It would not even be rape. 'For the last time Gail! Do you want me to have to get you into the car by force?'

She had smiled.

He had stifled his anxiety, tempered with pity. 'I mean . . . wake up your mother. Let her know . . . I believe she's elderly. Do you want that?'

His thoughts ran ahead. It would be so easy to stay here, to satisfy her and gratify himself. It had been so long . . .

She had started to put on her coat.

Fool, he had chided himself. Anyone who would go to such lengths, exhibit herself like someone pictured on a newsagent's top shelf, might still accuse him. 'We'll talk things over in the morning, Gail,' he had said evenly, 'When we're less tired, more ourselves.'

He knew exactly what he would do then. Perhaps she would not come to work, and he would be spared the unpleasantness; any embarrassment on possible charges of unfair dismissal. Either way, losing her expert assistance would be temporarily inconvenient.

Now, he tapped the desk with his fingers. He had thought that when she realised she had overstepped the mark last night, she would be really sorry. And depending on how sorry, and if it seemed unlikely ever to occur again, he would make light of the incident. Dismiss it, laugh it off, pretend he too must have had too much to drink, let her save face, and stay if she wished.

He continued to tap the desk. This morning, Gail Roberts had arrived, punctual as usual, as if nothing had happened. He had seen her with fresh eyes; noted her pathetic attempts at sophistication. The straight black hair and geometrically cut fringe. The eyeliner extended beyond her eyes in an upward sweep; a stereotyped picture of Cleopatra. And a low-cut blouse, wasted with no cleavage to reveal.

He had endured an unpleasant half-hour. 'We've no need to part bad friends, Gail, just because I don't want you in my bed. I'll give you a good reference.' She had accused him of leading her on, buying her drinks at the Sports Club, giving her lifts to the church for bell-ringing practice.

109

He had let her down, played fast and loose with her emotions, was carrying on with a married woman when, now that he was free, she had thought things between them would not only go on, but . . .

What things? He saw, in retrospect, the signs he had missed. The flowers, the fussing, the occasional skittish behaviour which, to spare her feelings, he had let pass without comment, and had thought, anyway, that if fussing around gave her pleasure . . . Now he realised it was he who, in turn, had been naive. Blind. Too amiable. If he had known what was really going on in her mind, he wouldn't have wasted time feeling slightly sorry for her; she had no boyfriend and the years were passing. God! For Heaven's sake – that Gail had ever imagined for one moment that there was ever a chance for her with him. She had even put the wrong interpretation on his calls to Helena, interrupting them with cups of coffee so she could listen to everything he said.

His hand moved involuntarily towards the phone beside him, then away. Now, more than ever, he ached to hear Helena's comforting voice. She had been especially sweet and understanding, only last Friday. But now she needed comfort herself. He had done his inadequate best in a letter.

Sighing, he flicked over the desk calendar to Monday, 25th March. What a way to start the week. So much on his mind, that his head felt like bursting. And now a depleted staff. Gail had gone. But he had a heavy feeling that this was not the end.

He started. The phone was ringing. He picked it up. 'Ian Price, estate agent.'

'Good afternoon, Mr Price. Detective Chief Inspector Robeson, here, CID. Could you come up to Police Headquarters? When you close will do. I'd just like a word.'

Ian hesitated. 'Er, yes. I can. Of course. Certainly. I'll look in.'

He had not thought despondency could sink much lower. He looked at his watch. Four o'clock. He might as well get it over. Sooner the better. He couldn't concentrate on things here now – property, surveys, and which of his staff was going to take Gail's place. Nothing mattered. *Bloody Hell,* he was going to be charged with *rape.*

Chapter 10

'Thank you for coming, sir.' Robeson led Ian Price away from the Incident Room where he had reported, and on to his own den on the third floor. 'I didn't expect you quite so promptly.' He scraped a chair from under the desk, indicating one on the other side: 'Business quiet? Blasted high mortgages?'

Price sat down. 'It was nearly time to pack up, anyway.'

Robeson liked saving time. Punctual interviewees started him off in the best mood whatever was to follow. This man was not even suspect.

'Mr Price. What I just want to know is, where were you on Saturday? What did you do?' He stopped short; his questions often caused twitching face muscles, and knuckles to be clenched white. But he was surprised to see this big hand-some man turn pale and his mouth fall open. He waited a moment, then prompted amiably: 'It's only two days ago.'

'I wasn't expecting . . .'

Robeson regarded him keenly. Here was someone every-body called a very nice chap; probably a wow with the ladies; the neat moustache, and sideburns; you didn't see many these days. And he was showing all the signs of guilt.

'What were you expecting?'

Price shrugged: 'Oh . . . well . . . I don't know.' He seemed to recover himself from some initial shock. 'Then, may I ask why I'm here?'

'Quite simply, Mr Price, as I said, I'd like to know where you were, or went, on Saturday.'

Price hesitated. 'Let's see. For the moment my mind's gone blank.' He shifted his big frame in the small chair to a more comfortable position.

'What do you usually do on a Saturday?' Robeson prompted courteously. 'Perhaps that'll help. I mean, for instance, do you go shopping? Or do you play golf?'

'Quite often.'

'Which? Shopping, or golf?'

'Perhaps . . . Sometimes both.'

'For instance, did you play golf on this Saturday just gone?' Robeson gave him time to think.

'No. Not this Saturday. I didn't play.'

Robeson had taken it for granted he had. 'Well, what did you do?'

Price made eye contact. 'Where exactly is this leading, officer? I don't understand. Why am I here being asked these questions?'

Robeson shifted his gaze to some papers in front of him and spoke lightly. 'You needn't sound mystified, Mr Price. For the moment it's just routine. You may be able to help us.'

'I can't see how.' Price crossed his long legs. 'I didn't do anything in particular. Nothing important.'

'What would you call not important?'

Price waited for Robeson to look up, then met his eyes. 'I really don't care for this, officer. I don't see why it's any business of yours, unless I'm told why.'

Robeson had simply wanted Price to confirm he had been in Links Road around lunchtime; then to ask him if he had seen anyone, a stranger, or anyone who appeared to be behaving suspiciously. Price's evasion was unexpected, and Robeson was curious. He knew the estate agent's good reputation, but fragments of personal information had seeped through intelligence, and the grapevine. Some of them might fit to form a picture. He continued lightly, 'I didn't intend to keep you long, Mr Price. But Saturday is only the day before yesterday. Surely you can remember?'

Price uncrossed his legs. 'Of course I can remember. But officer, it's so unimportant, I can't see what it's got to do with anything. And if you won't tell me what purpose . . .'

'We can skip the domestic bits. What time did you go out, say, in your car?'

'About . . . about eleven o'clock.'

'Where did you go?'

'To St Mark's Church.'

'Links Road?'

'That's right.'

'Any special reason? A service, or to attend a grave?'

'I gave one of my staff a lift. She's a bell ringer.'

Robeson played with a pencil. 'Was that arranged beforehand? Or did you pick her up by chance along the road?'

'I called for her. Well, not actually. She lives in a bungalow about two hundred yards from mine.'

'What d'you mean, not actually?'

'I stopped in her gateway. I usually toot, if her mother's not sitting in the window.'

'And did you? Was she?'

'Yes. She waved.'

'And this person on your staff, what is she called?'

'Miss Roberts.'

'You drove her to St Mark's Church about eleven. Any particular reason?'

'She asked me.'

Robeson smiled. 'Do you usually do what members of your staff ask you to?'

'No, officer, I don't. But she happens to live near, or at least, on my route if I'm playing golf.'

114

Robeson was surprised by the defensive tone. 'But you said you didn't play.'

'I didn't then, but I usually do. So I'd promised her, seeing as she'd asked.'

'Any particular reason why you decided against golf on Saturday?'

Price shrugged. 'I probably wasn't feeling too good.'

'Did you have something else on your mind?'

'Quite possibly.'

'Such as anything troubling you?'

'I don't know what you're getting at.'

Robeson adopted his impromptu tone to sound affable while winkling out what he wanted to know. He had not intended to take this line, to delve deeper, until pushed by the man's evasion. 'Well, I take it you felt well enough to take Miss Roberts to the church?'

'I'd said that I would, and I don't let people down. Apparently there was a wedding.'

Robeson scratched his chin. He liked Price's modulated voice. 'What did you do after you dropped Miss Roberts at the church?'

'I went home.'

'Did you stay there for the rest of the day?'

'Officer, I lost my wife less than a month ago. I've plenty to do.'

'Yes, Mr Price. Of course. I'm sorry.' Robeson paused to show his respect. He continued courteously, 'And I'm very sorry that this seems to be upsetting you. But it would help if you would simply answer my questions.' He knew, if Lady Glen-Esk's information was correct, that Price had gone out again. It dawned on him why. 'Of course, I suppose you had to pick up Miss Roberts after the wedding?'

Price did not answer.

Robeson waited. His remark required a simple yes. He

could then ask Price if he had seen anyone or anything unusual at the far end of Links Road.

Price said, 'No, I didn't pick her up.'

'You didn't?' Robeson, jolted from his assumption, cocked a questioning eyebrow.

'No, officer. Should I have?'

Robeson did not answer.

Price went on, 'Actually, I did offer, but she didn't know what time. She said she'd make her own way home.'

Robeson drummed the table with his thick fingers. 'In that case, Mr Price, what took you to the end of Links Road at around twelve-thirty, or thereabouts?'

Price's eyes widened. He straightened up and faced Robeson squarely. 'I think . . .' He paused: 'I do believe I see now. I know what you're getting at.' He paused again. 'Would this questioning be anything to do with the terrible tragedy?'

'You admit you were in the vicinity?'

'But good grief . . . ! You surely don't think . . . ?'

'Were you in the vicinity?'

'Yes.'

'All I wanted to know, Mr Price, when I asked you here, was whether you saw anything unusual? Or anyone behaving suspiciously.'

'Couldn't you have come to the point right away?'

'I wanted you to tell me you were there, first, Mr Price.' Robeson ran his hand back through his hair. 'I like people to tell me where they were, and what they were doing, when I ask them. I don't put words in their mouths.' He had not expected this interview to go like this. Price was one of the most respected businessmen in the area. Nevertheless, Robeson knew the world was full of the unexpected. 'Well, now that we have got to the point, did you see anything, or anyone?'

Price shook his head: 'No, and I've thought about it a lot since I heard the terrible news. I've tried to think back.'

'Well, Mr Price, since it seems you were not going to tell me you were in the area, perhaps you'll tell me what you were doing there?'

'It has absolutely no relevance.'

'Did you see anything at all?'

'No.'

'But surely something. Did you see a car? Or anyone perhaps walking their dog?'

Price did not answer.

'You hadn't played golf, nor come out to take Miss Roberts home. But you were seen outside The Firs.'

'It had absolutely nothing to do with the tragedy.'

'Well, in that case perhaps you can tell me why you were there.'

'It was something personal. Nothing to do with what happened.'

'What had happened? Or was to happen?'

Price slotted his long sensitive fingers into cat's cradle. 'Officer, I didn't know anything had happened. I simply wanted to see Mrs Bray.'

'A business call?'

'No.'

Robeson raised his eyebrows and waited.

'I wanted to give her something.'

Robeson waited again; he often learnt a lot from silence.

Price said, eventually, 'It was nothing much.' He added reluctantly, 'Just a gesture of thanks.'

Robeson reflected on whispers on the grapevine. Casual remarks dropped by business colleagues; Price was sweet on Helena Bray. 'Thanks? For what?'

'Really, officer! It has absolutely nothing to do with this.'

'Mr Price, I can only agree, or otherwise, if I'm told what it did have to do with.'

Price examined his finger nails. 'Mrs Bray was particularly kind and understanding, after I lost my wife.'

'So you were going to give her a gift?'

'Hardly that, officer. A mere gesture, no monetary value. She could have bought it herself.'

'Won't you tell me what it was?'

'It's irrelevant.'

Robeson waited, his eyebrow cocked. He wondered if Price, seemingly drawn into himself, was deciding the nature of the gift, or on whether to impart the information

'It was simply a cassette,' Price said grudgingly at last. 'Mozart Horn Concertos.'

Robeson recalled his interview with Mrs Bray. He smiled. 'Mrs Bray likes Mozart, does she?'

'We both do.'

Robeson had intended this interview to be short and friendly. He had deviated only because of Price's odd reaction to his first question, and subsequent deliberate evasion. 'So you're a friend of the Brays?'

'Not really. Not close. I've done business with Bray, and I occasionally go there to dinner.'

'So you knew Mrs Bray's sister?'

'A sweet girl.'

'How do you think they got on? I mean Mr Bray and his sister-in-law?' Robeson knew, according to Julie the cook, that Bray had been overheard to say he would have been glad to be shot of her.

'All right, I think.'

'I understand she had some sort of disability. Did he seem to resent her at all?'

'Officer, I don't accept hospitality, and then discuss my host.'

Robeson rolled a pencil between his thumb and forefinger. He was dealing with no fool. 'Very commendable. Incidentally, what time did you give this . . . er . . . cassette to Mrs Bray?'

'I didn't give it to her.'

'After going out especially to do so?'

Price said nothing.

'Did you intend to give it to her? Did you slow up at her drive?'

'Er . . . Yes.'

'What made you change your mind about taking it in to her?'

Price shrugged.

'But you did change your mind, and drive on?'

'Er . . . yes.'

'Why?'

Price shrugged again. 'I just did.'

'Was it because you saw Mr Bray's car in the drive? And you thought he had gone away?'

Price flushed. 'Possibly.'

'Come, Mr Price. We're both men of the world. Was that the case or not?'

'Yes. But look, officer, what's all this leading to? Do you think I shot Mrs Bray's sister?'

'Mr Price, I can't even begin to imagine that you would.' He paused. He had known of stranger things. It seemed inconceivable that Price was in the vicinity within an hour of the tragedy, yet could not supply a lead. 'Did you think that if you gave Mrs Bray the cassette in front of her husband, he might . . . well . . . resent it, or perhaps pull her leg?'

'I suppose that's the long and short of it. He's a funny man.'

Robeson knew the remark had slipped out. 'Is he jealous?'

'I don't know about that.'

'Are you fond of Mrs Bray?' Robeson knew he was going wide, but minute details, and background, sometimes joined to make sense.

'I admire her. She's naturally kind and sympathetic. I doubt she knows how I feel about her.'

119

'How do you feel?'

'I've just said.'

Robeson drew his own conclusions. There had been whispers. 'When you drew up at the drive, what exactly did you see?'

'Only Mr Bray's car parked inside.'

'Was Mr Bray in his car? Or in the drive?'

'I didn't stop to notice. I drove straight on.'

'So you didn't see anyone?'

'No.'

'Not even an elderly lady with a dog?'

'I don't think so, I went on quickly.'

Robeson put down his pencil and tapped his fingers on the table. That tied up. But there had been something odd about Price's reaction when he arrived. 'What time was this?'

'I can't be exact. Half past twelve, quarter to one-ish.'

'Did you see anything? Meet anyone at all?'

'I don't think so.'

'I mean anywhere? For instance, further down Links Road as you drove on quickly, presumably to go home?'

'I wasn't taking any notice.'

Robeson fixed his eyes on Price. 'Did you see our cars? Our officers flying up through? Two tones going?'

Price hesitated. 'Come to think of it. I did see a lot of traffic. Up the other end by the church.' He stroked his sideburns. 'And I do remember, now, hearing a police car.'

Robeson was surprised anyone could forget that in a hurry; the peace of Links Road wasn't shattered every day with the blare of two tones. He had not fathomed Price – his nervousness when he had arrived at the Incident Room, his sudden pallor when first questioned, and his subsequent yarn about a gift for Mrs Bray. Perhaps it was cock and bull. But he had no reason to detain him. He stood up. 'Well thank you very much, Mr Price. I hope I haven't wasted too much of your time.' Accompanying him towards the door, he said casually: 'This little gift . . .'

'I've still got it. Perhaps one day, when she's got over this.' Price produced the tape from his jacket pocket. Mozart Horn Concertos.

Robeson had pinned his hopes on Price providing a lead; the estate agent had been near the scene of the crime almost within an hour of when it must have occurred. But he had revealed nothing, apart from his admiration of Mrs Bray.

Frustrated, Robeson looked at the big round clock on the office wall. Time to get home or there would be another meal spoilt. Not that Janet expected him to work gentlemen's hours; but he had told her that for the time being, he might just as well. He had reached stalemate, trying to solve this murder. What was the motive? If only he could discover a motive.

He made his way down two flights of stone stairs. His work, as Janet so often chided him, was his addiction; he sometimes wanted to kick it, yet couldn't let go. Passing the Incident Room he took a last peep in. Every big case pulled him like a jigsaw lying half done; he couldn't pass without seeing if just another piece fitted.

A number of DCs, submerged in paperwork, were still on shifts. They studied files, and manned phones. Between crowded desks waste-paper bins overflowed with empty crisp bags, and carton evidence of consumed Kentucky chicken. Robeson noted that the usual life and soul of the party, Sergeant Roger Mills, had left. But they were still a good bunch here. Little of the perpetual snarling between ranks as depicted on television: Super bites Inspector, Inspector bites sergeant, sergeant bites constable. It didn't happen in his Division, and if it did, he would want to know why.

He glanced over the heads. Occasional snaps were inevitable but, in his opinion, if coppers behaved as on television they would never turn up for duty in the first place. Not if they had any sense. He called to no one in particular: 'Anything new in the past half-hour?'

There was no enthusiasm in the eyes that looked up.

'You're probably all as baffled as I am. On the face of it, what have we got? A madman with a gun that he's probably hung on to and disappeared. But where?' Robeson paced the room, in his zeal momentarily forgetting that waiting for him at home was one of Janet's superb meals. 'A prowler. A nut case. Our best hope is that someone will cough the job.' Leaving, he added, 'We're only as good as our informants.'

He told himself most of his informants were men he had locked up. But men he had treated right; men he had helped occasionally; done this and that for, taken messages to wives and girlfriends. Admittedly, it was help he had sometimes given with an ulterior motive.

In his book, everything hung on motive. Yet what possible motive could there have been for shooting a young woman in the back? It was not a sexual motive. Was the motive the kick derived from a shoot-and-run? Or could it have been a wish to exterminate someone whose existence created a problem?

In his mind, he recapped on what he had asked Price: 'Are you fond of Mrs Bray?

'I admire her.'

Robeson had read more into that. The grapevine supported it. But that was a different matter. Or was it? He had seen all the signs of a man in love with another man's wife. Had Price been thinking forward and decided the girl would be in the way, an encumbrance? Would Price, like Bray, have liked to be rid of her?

It did not fit. Absurd. But sometimes Robeson let his

mind whirl, let it scratch at anything. Returning to normality, he knew that if Bray resented the murdered girl, no other decent human being would. And Price, from all reports, was an impeccable character. Being in love with another man's wife was nothing extraordinary. It happened every day. It certainly was not a crime.

Chapter 11

Robeson perused the door-to-door enquiry reports. Surrounded by paper, four days after the murder, he was irked still to be without a lead. He had pinned hopes on yesterday's interview, sure that Price would have seen someone, or have noticed something untoward, or could have pointed a finger at someone with a motive.

With nothing forthcoming, Robeson knew he had clutched at straws; wisps of information that on the face of things for the moment, had nothing to do with the case. Even the Super's briefing this morning had lacked fire, and forwarded nothing new. There had been no need for him to tell the men to remember their training; to persuade an interviewee to a particular course of action; make him decide to confide in you; and note signals – like his asking you to repeat the question, so he can think.

Robeson did not deny Moore was a good copper. But after the briefing, and yet another press conference, he had actually digressed when they were alone, and bellyached the now stale news that his wife had left him. Such a waste of good detection time – and then expecting a bloody progress report. Robeson wanted a breakthrough, and a result. He pushed the files aside, and went downstairs.

In the Incident Room, he leaned his large frame against a table. It was a spacious, impersonal office shared by sergeants and constables alike, all on first-name terms. As always, most were immersed in paperwork, ignoring the general buzz around them – the banter, and exchanged views, phones ringing and being answered. Desk tops were buried beneath files and forms, ashtrays were full, waste-paper baskets overflowed.

Robeson sensed enthusiasm. 'Anything new?' he asked the room in general. 'Anything worth reading aloud?'

Heads looked up. Sergeant Mills was first to speak, as usual, from his desk at the front. 'Yes, sir. Info from funny sources. Don't know where they'd fit. But several sightings of that car in Links Road.'

Robeson liked the slightly-built sergeant's unashamed beavering for promotion. 'Which car, Roger?'

'The green one, sir.'

'Not the cream one?'

'Nothing on that, sir. A green Ford, they think. But an Express milkman . . .' Mills consulted his notes, 'According to him, a green Mondeo, seen several times, being driven slowly. He reckoned the driver wasn't looking where he was going. He nearly collided with the milk float.'

'When?'

'Last Friday. And someone also reported seeing a green Ford in that area last week. Another was sure he'd seen a Mondeo.'

'Well, are we talking of one car? Or four different ones, Roger?'

'Who knows, sir? Most agree it was green, and timings seem to tally, more or less.'

'Anyone get the number?'

'No, sir. Two DCs are out to contact the milkman and hear what more he can cough up. People don't attach importance to seeing cars, not at the time.' He brightened: 'Only the fireman.'

'What fireman?'

'There was a house fire in Links Road, Friday.'

'What time?'

Mills read from his notes: 'We got the call at fifteen hundred hours. The fire service was at the scene within six minutes.'

'Well?' Robeson waited.

'Apparently, later, this fireman ticked off some bloke in a car. He was in the way of the hoses.'

'What did he say?'

'He told him to bugger on off, out of the way.'

'Well, Roger, I don't give a damn what he cussed. Did the fireman give you any description?'

'All he knew was, the man was in the bloody way. When I asked for a description, the fireman swore again and said he didn't take something notes – seeing as he was jammed in a bloody helmet and leggings, with steam rising from his sodden tunic.'

'Well, what time was this? You said "later".'

'He thinks about three-thirtyish; perhaps twenty to four.'

'Didn't he even look at the man he cussed?'

'Thinks he was possibly young. Pretty sure the car was a green Mondeo.'

'Huh. Mondeo again. Then use the Vehicle Index. Besides being cross-indexed on makes and colours, you'll find notes on who's currently using them.'

'Yes, sir.'

Robeson scanned the rest of his subordinates. He hoped the bright eyes would stay; he had seen too many men grow hard by unsocial hours, gruesome sights, and witnessing too often the worst side of human nature. 'What time were the other sightings?'

'They vary, sir. Morning, early lunch, some mid-afternoon. But always a green car, they think.'

Robeson grunted. 'It calls for our usual notice. Police anxious to hear from a man seen driving, etcetera etcetera, to eliminate him from our enquiries.'

126

Detective Constable Searle called from further back in the room: 'I've a report here, sir . . . A postman. Delivering Friday, Links Road. Sounds like same car – green.'

'You sound pleased, Mike. What's new?'

'Description of driver, sir. Fair hair, cut too short, sticking up.

'It'll be shoulder length if we don't get this wrapped up soon,' Mills said.

'Bloody right' Robeson muttered. Trust Roger Mills to come back with his two-penn'orth.

Searle said: 'He was wearing dark glasses. Outside The Firs, give or take a few yards.'

'Dark glasses, up there?' Robeson took heart. 'But the road's dismal. All those trees. You'd miss anyone walking on the path if you didn't have your eyes skinned.' Perhaps at last he would soon be thinking about the best order to interview suspects. 'Right, Mike' he called: 'Look up the ACI. And Street Index. See if there's a fella with hair like a scrubbing brush, going round in a green Mondeo.'

'Yes, sir.'

Robeson rested one buttock on the table, one leg dangling, one foot on the floor. Information was his stock in trade. It came over the telephone, on scraps of paper, as remarks mentioned in passing. He listened to further reports. Ideas and opinions soaked into his blotting-paper mind like ink, and were absorbed for keeps, while he, a scrooge for clues, gave nothing back. He turned to Mills. 'And your other gems, Roger?'

'There's a message for you to contact the matron of a Residential Home in Draymouth.'

Robeson cocked an eyebrow. 'Anything to do with this enquiry?'

'She wouldn't say, sir. Only that it wasn't urgent; least, she didn't think so. She said as you, that nice Inspector

Robeson, weren't here, p'raps you'd ring, or call to see her.'

'Mmm. Well . . .' Obviously someone who thought they knew him. 'What else?'

'Another special for you, sir. Contact Canadian Airlines. Maybe offering a free hol to the Rockies, and the Grand Canyon. However else would they fit?'

'It's our job to find out, Roger.'

Robeson had no idea. He was intrigued. He just hoped the contact would be more fruitful than the interview he had last evening with Ian Price.

Ian Price had put the interview out of his mind. It had irritated him as a waste of time, with six cats at home waiting to be fed, and a meal to prepare for himself. After that, he wanted to get to a rehearsal on time. As a change from his usual role of playing first violin, he was going to perform as solo tenor, enriched occasionally, he hoped, by a full chorus and orchestral accompaniment.

Nevertheless, throughout the evening, absorbed in Lehar's song poems from Paganini, and suffering the irony of singing 'Girls were made to love and kiss', which reminded him of Helena Bray, he had snatched grateful moments to reflect that the interview with Inspector Robeson at Headquarters had not been, as he had feared, to answer false charges of rape.

His peace of mind was short-lived. This morning, in his outer office, seated at her desk as usual, he had found Miss Roberts.

'Good morning, Mr Price.'

What a nerve. Back. Here. As if nothing had happened. Speechless, he regarded the cadaverous face, white as bleached flour; the crimson lips, and straight jet-black hair.

She said no more. He saw her hands moving with exaggerated adeptness over the keyboard of her computer, as if she were conducting a seance. She jerked the trunk of her body, alternately sticking her shoulders forward; miming, like some Marcel Marceau, that she was and intended to go on being busily engaged in her work.

He went into his own office and closed the door. At his desk, he leaned forward and held his head in his hands. So much for yesterday.

He had told her firmly, but nicely, it would be better for both of them if she looked for another job. He should have been much firmer. But he had wanted their parting to be if not friendly, then at least dignified. He had given her the chance to save face. She had clutched the lapels of his jacket: 'Oh no you don't! After three years! You've led me on, haven't you? And now when it's possible for you and me, I'm not good enough.'

He had contained his shock, removed her hands from around his neck where she had thrown them, and eased her eager body from pressing against his, and faced her. Her accusations were beyond his imagination. Surely he had never given her reason to believe that if he were not married . . . ? He had never touched her. Never knowingly encouraged her to think that if he were free . . .

He had said: 'I'll see you get everything, Gail. Your money. Your redundancy . . .'

'So you think you can buy me off? Just like that?'

'It is your legal due.'

'It's unfair dismissal after three years duty and devotion!'

'I'm sorry, Gail.'

She had narrowed her eyes beneath her straight fringe of black hair. 'You know I worship you!'

'Then it is far better you leave.'

Her thin lips had pressed against her teeth. She had hissed, 'But I found you out!'

He had clenched his fists to contain himself, her tone angered him as she went on giving him no chance to speak.

'You got rid of your wife, didn't you?'

The skin above his lips had stung with sweat; the woman was sick.

She began to cry. 'You're free. And you could have had me. Then I found out – that other woman!'

He contained his rage. Struggling to mask his discomfort as if he were accustomed to such a situation and in full command, he said, 'Please leave. Immediately.'

After several moments, she had left. He had assumed she had gone home. He had not expected to see her here this morning.

Now there was a tap on his door. He glanced up. 'Yes?'

Gail sidled in, closed the door behind her and stood with her back to it

'Yes Gail? What is it? I thought you had left.'

She said, 'I'm sorry.'

He waited, unprepared.

'I would like to stay, please. I am very sorry. For everything.'

He felt a crawl of sympathy. It was no good. She spelt danger. He had seen and heard it.   'Well, thank you, Gail. I do accept your apology.' He tapped his long sensitive fingers on the desk; he had not been ready for any of this. 'But I think perhaps . . .' He thought quickly. 'How about a holiday? I've seen you have three weeks due.'

'I don't want it, I wouldn't see you.'

'You would have time to think things over. Perhaps you'd meet someone, you never know.' It was a remote hope. Irrationally, he felt responsible for her mental state. But at least she had not accused him of rape. Perhaps he had misjudged her.

She sniffed. 'All right.'

He watched her go. Three weeks' breathing space. Then

he would have to terminate her employment once and for all. He would miss her efficiency; another of his staff would have to improve their computer skills. But never again would he allow anyone to fill his precious desk space with bowls of flowers. Today, at least, they had not been rearranged or added to, and Gail Roberts would not be here to keep buzzing in to give them fresh water.

He glanced at a vase of early daffodils which, like chrysanthemums, were in his opinion better kept outdoors, but these could stay till they died. You did not chuck out babies because their mother displeased you.

He referred to his appointment book; he had to survey and value a large property, some miles out. He was reminded of the last occasion when on similar business he had taken Gail to assist him. It had been a long morning. On the way back, to avoid the lunchtime traffic in town, he had stopped at a pub, sixteenth-century, with low ceiling and beams, tankards and hunting horns, horse brasses and pistols. Outside, the branches of a tree curled round the little leaded windows.

'Isn't it romantic, Ian?'

Only very occasionally did Gail call him Ian. He had chosen not to notice.

'I think it's really romantic,' she had repeated, as excited as a child. 'Such a lovely old tree.'

He had said, 'The roots must be playing hell with the drains. And it makes the place dark.'

'But Ian, the walls – that lovely red creeper!'

He had said, 'If they don't watch it, it'll weaken the mortar.'

Now, thinking back as he fingered his appointment book, he realised he should have seen the signs then. He tapped his fingers on the desk. He needed someone to talk to. He would miss his daily few words with Helena. He had sent his written condolences after the tragedy, and received her note of thanks in return. But she had asked for nothing more, no daily few minutes on the phone as he had asked of her after he lost Carol.

He had treasured those moments. Dark, and secret; all his own. They soothed him, then filled him with guilt. He had found himself comparing two women, thinking what might have been. He, and Helena Bray. Soul in her brown eyes. Chestnut hair that as she moved, flickered and glinted like flames from a coal fire. Instead, what had been? Life with Carol. Dead eyes, uncombed hair, a grubby dressing gown. Carol's days punctuated by feeding six spoilt cats. Six cats with silly names. Carol who neglected everything and everyone, including herself, but rang the vet any minute of the day or night if one of the cats had a dry nose.

He felt in his jacket pocket. The cassette for Helena was still there. But now Mozart's Horn Concertos did not seem right.

He wanted to see her. He remembered the look in her eyes when they had met his over their glasses of wine. He thought he had seen the hurt inflicted by Laurence, the disgust she felt for his friend Neville, and the sisterly bond for Annaliese. He had not dared to hope there was anything there for him. And yet . . . 'We all have our crosses', he had said as he thanked her and wished her good night.

She had not withdrawn her hand from his as soon as she could have.

Perhaps now, if she was not still too devastated, she would not mind too much if he enquired how she was, in person, at The Firs.

Chapter 12

Robeson had intended to wait before going back to The Firs. Since he had called on Saturday, finding Laurence Bray anaesthetised with whisky and his wife devastated and only half aware of what was going on, it had seemed right and proper to allow more time for their grief and shock to settle.

But it was now time for a word. And he was glad Bray had agreed to come to Divisional Headquarters, rather than be visited in his own office or at The Firs. It was hardly surprising. Bray often came here in his role of solicitor, so the place was not as awesome to him as it sometimes seemed to be for the man in the street.

Robeson studied the statement in front of him. Mrs Bray had told the scene-of-crime officer that she had come out of the front door and started to descend the flight of stone steps. At the same time, Mr Bray had driven into the drive. From their different viewpoints they saw, lying close to the foot of the steps, the body of Mrs Bray's sister, Miss Annaliese Meade.

Straightforward enough, Robeson mused. But it was always his policy to hear statements repeated straight from the horse's mouth. And now it seemed a still better time; the intervening days had been charged with whispers, rumours and diverse facts from unexpected quarters.

He surveyed the paperwork on his desk, organised with

relevant files at hand. He liked his office entirely functional, with a masculine disregard for fripperies. The pale emulsioned walls were enlivened with nothing more than filing cabinets, reference books, occasional posters for wanted persons and suchlike. His one concession to personalisation was a framed photo of Janet beside the phone. And that, he told himself, despite his regard for her, was there more to satisfy the whim of his teenage daughter than any desire of his own.

He looked up in response to a brief tap on the door. DC Searle looked in. 'Mr Bray, sir.'

Robeson half rose from his chair, indicating one on the other side of his desk. 'Good morning, Mr Bray. Take a seat.'

Bray was ebullient. 'And how can I help you, officer? I made a full statement on Saturday.'

'Yes. I know. Thank you. And how is your wife bearing up?'

'Pretty well, I suppose. She did go to pieces at first.'

'Understandable,' Robeson muttered.

Bray sounded in full command. 'I told her she wants to pull herself together. Are you getting anywhere, officer? Anything to report? It's five days now.'

Robeson never answered questions. 'Rest assured, Mr Bray, everything's being done. Stops pulled out.' He gauged the solicitor was about his own age; possibly a few years younger, but the heavy jowl didn't help. And in Bray's profession, the elements could hardly be blamed for staining his nose and complexion with red veins; they probably owed more to whisky.

'Then, officer, in what way can I help you?'

Robeson noted the broad forehead, and wondered if the receding hairline was a threat to vanity. The man had strutted into the room, making an exaggerated effort to push back his shoulders and diminish his midriff: 'Mr Bray, did your sister-in-law enjoy good health?'

'Oh yes, apart from being deaf, and unable to speak very well. And she was slightly lame.'

'Did you get on well with her?'

'Of course.'

'And your wife did too?'

'Inseparable. They were twins you know.'

Robeson stroked his chin. Bray had a certain deceitful charm. As if determined to appear young and trendy, he was wearing a mauve silk shirt with an open collar. It looked all wrong for him. 'Can you think of anyone who would have wished to harm your wife's sister?'

'Absolutely no one.'

Robeson kept his voice friendly and matter-of-fact. 'Is it true, Mr Bray, that you are leaving England next month for Canada?' He did not miss Bray's slight twitch, his momentary hesitation.

'That is so.'

Robeson feigned surprise. 'But you have such a good practice.'

Bray looked smug. 'The best, but I mustn't get in a rut.'

Robeson stroked his chin.

Bray said, 'I foresee opportunities in Canada.'

Robeson nodded, as if he agreed that was good. He said casually, 'So your wife and her sister were twins?'

'Yes.'

'That's interesting. And inseparable?'

'Absolutely.'

Robeson slowly tapped his fingers together as if he were doing a soft clap. He wanted to keep his tone friendly, with a natural curiosity that did not sound like interrogation. 'Well, Mr Bray, if they were inseparable, why were you going to Canada without her?'

Bray shifted and straightened up. 'Officer, I don't think personal, family matters, need come into this, do you? We had our reasons, my wife and I.'

'Of course.' Robeson knew the signs. The man was touchy. 'Did you find a place for her sister in a Residential Home?'

'I did, actually. A very nice place.'

'I see.' Robeson had only asked what he knew to be true. Bray would have recognised that, and been too intelligent to deny it. 'Did your wife want to go to Canada?'

'Of course.'

'And leave her sister?'

'I pointed out it was kinder not to take Annaliese away from everything she knew.'

'Did your wife agree?'

'Of course.'

'Wasn't she in the least upset?'

'Perhaps a bit, naturally, at first. But I said to her, I said: you want to snap out of it, Helena. You don't want to get in a rut; spend the rest of your life in a one-horse town.'

Robeson nodded as if he understood. 'Did you decide about Canada . . . I mean . . . before consulting her?'

'There was no need.'

Robeson cocked an eyebrow.

'I know my wife. She does what I want.'

'Did she really want to go to Canada?'

'Well, officer, she did and she didn't. You know women.'

'Did you have to win her round?'

'Have you been listening to tittle-tattle?'

'Did she agree to go if her sister went too?'

'That's quite right. But officer, this has absolutely nothing to do with my sister-in-law's murder. Who's been gossiping?'

'Is it true you have two flight seats reserved?'

'Quite true.'

'Why not three?'

Bray hesitated. 'Well . . . I hadn't had time yet . . .'

Robeson made eye contact and waited.

Bray glanced away. 'I suppose, really, I was still hoping to persuade my wife her sister would be better off here.'

'Could you possibly have foreseen that Annaliese wouldn't be around?'

Bray stood up, his face puce. 'How could I possibly have known?'

'Keep calm, Mr Bray.'

'You know I had nothing to do with her death.'

'It appears you didn't. But please sit down.'

'Is this the friendly man-to-man chat that you suggested we had?' Bray plonked back down in his chair. 'You're supposed to be looking for a murderer, officer, not poking your nose into people's private affairs. I came to hear what you've been doing this past five days.'

Robeson stayed calm. 'Well, for starters, my men haven't been sitting on their arses all day.'

'Seems like it.'

'We're making enquiries. Following every avenue. But you should know, Mr Bray, perhaps more than anyone – when you go fishing, you sometimes dredge more than you expect.'

Bray glowered. 'I thought you were conducting a murder enquiry, not doing a column for the damn News of the World.'

'Can we get back to why you have two flight seats booked for mid-April?'

'I told you, I was still hoping to persuade my wife what was best for her sister.'

'And you still kept open the place you'd booked for her sister, in the Residential Home?'

'Yes.'

Robeson tapped his thick fingers on the papers in front of him. 'It's Wednesday . . .' He quietly stated the obvious while thinking how best to ease himself onto a different tack. He said, 'On Monday, did your secretary suddenly leave your employ?'

Bray glowered. 'Just what has that got to do with you, or any of this?'

'Did she tell you she wouldn't go to Canada with you as you'd planned?'

Bray gulped. Speechless, his jowls squared.

Robeson said, 'Had news of the murder shocked her?'

Bray found his voice. 'Shocked everyone, didn't it?'

'How long had your secretary been with you?'

Bray shrugged. 'About twelve months. She's a flighty young madam. Unreliable. You can't believe . . .'

'Had you and she . . . I think it's described these days as . . . formed a relationship?'

'I've said she was unreliable. You can't take any notice of what she says.'

'Do you deny you were attracted?' Robeson noted Bray's seeming reluctance to answer. 'Attracted because she's young? And very pretty?'

Bray said grudgingly: 'Well perhaps a little at first. You know how it is.'

'Did she end your affair with her on Monday, as a direct result of hearing about the murder?'

Bray was silent.

'Because she was frightened?'

Bray didn't answer.

Robeson cut into his thinking. 'Mr Bray. Was that second air booking for your secretary?'

Bray pressed his forehead with a clean white handkerchief.

Robeson had the information, even if Bray was not going to substantiate it. 'Mr Bray, as that second ticket was for your young secretary, and Miss Annaliese Meade had a place waiting for her in a Home . . . ?'

Bray scowled into his lap and wiped the back his neck.

Robeson said, 'Where did that leave your wife? Alone? Back at The Firs?'

Wearily Bray put his handkerchief away and leaned on the desk. 'Officer, you said we'd have a man-to-man chat. I object to being treated as a suspect.'

'We have to check every scrap of information we get. And you're not immune from the law, Mr Bray, even if you do know better than most how it works.'

'But why my private affairs? All this irrelevance? I don't understand how any of this . . .'

'Neither do I, Mr Bray. I was just hoping perhaps you could help.'

'But officer, you're meant to be looking for a murderer. I don't even possess a gun.'

Robeson tapped the table. No, he could not see any daylight here. He could only smell fish. He spoke leisurely, as if nothing said had been of much importance. 'I'm just trying to do a job.' He paused: 'Do you know of anyone who does possess a gun who would be likely . . . ?'

'Absolutely no one.'

'Then it seems the work of some thug. No rhyme nor reason. But we'll get the bugger.'

An orderly brought in two cups of coffee. Robeson grinned. 'Usually a mug when I'm on my own.' He took a few sips and set the cup down. He glanced at Bray. 'You're not a stranger to tragedy, are you?'

'I've had my share.' Bray sounded less buoyant than when he arrived.

'A fire, wasn't it? Five years ago?'

'A dreadful accident. On Guy Fawkes night.'

Robeson drank his coffee and allowed Bray time to finish his. Casually, he said, 'I seem to remember. What exactly . . . ?'

'I'd bought an old chalet at Draymouth, overlooking the cliffs. I thought it'd be a good place for weekends.'

Robeson knew that part. The tarted-up shack built mostly of wood, and well insured.

Bray said, 'We used calor gas up there to make tea. Cylinder must've been leaking. Probably a worn washer.'

'Didn't you have a paraffin stove, too?'

'Yes. For warmth. Well ... that evening when my wife went up it was November.'

Robeson nodded: 'And it was then you lost your wife?'

'Yes. It was terrible. She'd arranged a barbecue, you know. For some kiddies.'

Robeson effected a look of deep sympathy. 'Who were they?'

'Don't know. But they had a lucky escape.'

Robeson recalled he had heard of no parents, at the time, thanking God that the fire happened before their children had arrived at the party.

'My wife had lots of fireworks ready. Then who knows what happened? Must've got the barbecue going.'

Robeson always maintained that not even a chalet goes up like that by accident.

Bray tutted. 'I suppose, then, being bonfire night and the place out of the way, no one took notice till too late.'

Robeson remembered the all-consuming inescapable blaze.

Bray said: 'I blamed the Fire Service. Took ages to get there.'

Robeson did not want to hear what he had heard before. He had reckoned the excuses stank. 'The lads would've done their usual good job, given half a chance.'

Bray repeated what was already recorded: 'It looked like just simply another fifth of November. The result of a rocket thrown. It was thought the place was unoccupied.'

'With a paraffin stove going like a bomb? Evidence of paraffin spilt all round outside in the grass?'

'My dear wife was doing a kindness for the kiddies. That

was the only inside heating she had. She was apt to be careless.'

'Who told the firemen the place was empty?'

Bray looked innocent, shaking his head. 'I wasn't there.'

'The lads might've got to your wife in time. And not stamped their big boots all over the scene.'

'They hadn't dreamed that anyone like my dear wife . . .'

Robeson thought angrily it was still his belief that five years ago, someone had got away with murder. He looked hard at Bray. 'And do you really think the fire was an accident?'

'Oh, undoubtedly. It was the general opinion my wife must have spilt paraffin when she carried in a new can to fill up the stove. Then someone up there, skylarking up on the hill, had thrown a rocket.'

Robeson stroked his chin. He would let Bray think he had swallowed the yarns, as others had at the time. Feeble tales of how fortunate it was that the children's invitations had been mislaid and not sent. 'Damn fireworks. Should be banned.' He knew that by even broaching the subject, he had made Bray uneasy. Well, let him sweat a bit. He stood up. 'Thank you very much, Mr Bray, for coming along. You have been very helpful.'

He allowed himself a satisfied smile. He thought: and if I can never get him for having his first wife roasted alive, or for this latest murder, at least I would love to see his podgy, self-satisfied mug when he discovers that for a long time the Fraud Squad has been sitting on his tail.

Chapter 13

Robeson had faith in the Fraud Squad. He could hardly wait for detectives to swoop on Laurence Bray. He had been under surveillance long enough.

It was Bray's young wife that Robeson felt sorry for. She probably knew nothing of some of her husband's so-called business activities: land deals that collapsed when planning applications were turned down; his attempted share frauds in Government sell-offs; his clients' money used for his own stock market schemes. It was also unlikely that she knew of her husband's infidelity. And she might never have found out, until too late, if her sister had not been murdered.

The murder had scared Bray's young secretary. Their planned flit to Canada was one thing. Murder was another. She obviously thought this murder appeared too close to Laurence and his conniving to be coincidental.

In her panic, she had not only let him know the whole thing was off, she had released a load of creepy-crawlies from out of the woodwork. And unexpectedly, Fraud Squad investigators, long hesitant in the wings like actors waiting to make certain they had got everything right before going on stage, had got their break.

Robeson sighed. Lucky dogs. What he could just do with a stroke of chance like that. He had a murder to solve. And the CID could plod on for months, and come up with nothing.

He went down to the Incident Room. Even there he could detect less buzz, less enthusiasm, the boredom of stalemate. He glanced at heads bent over reports, or engrossed in cross-referencing statements. His eyes rested on Mary Starks. 'Inspector, I'd like you to come with me. We'll go along to The Firs to see Mrs Bray.'

He wondered how Mrs Bray was bearing up. He hoped the first shock was over; perhaps now she could give him some ideas. But any policeman who said he had got used to murder, or other people's grief, was either a liar or made of stone: 'It's just routine, Mary. In our role of PR officers.'

Down in the car park, he gave Inspector Starks the nod to take the wheel of the car.

'Does Mrs Bray know we are coming, sir?'

'Yes. And we should find her alone. At least, without him.' He had taken the trouble to find out. He did not want to see Bray, with so much pending. It was better that Bray had no inkling of how the net was closing round him; or how many beans had been spilled from his secretarial can. For the time being, he could go on patting himself on the back.

'Some difference from Monday, sir. I wonder if Lady Glen-Esk's porch has dried out.'

'Glen-Esk with a hyphen,' Robeson drawled. He liked Mary's driving. It was smooth, and he could relax for five minutes.

She turned out of the tarmac square that was the Headquarters car park, and made for the main road before turning off towards the avenues. The Firs, beyond St Mark's Church in Links Road, was less than ten minutes away.

It was good to be out of the office. With little breeze, and hardly a cloud in the sky, it promised to be a perfect spring day. At The Firs, Helena Bray opened the front door herself.

Robeson noted the small, sad smile. 'This is Inspector Mary Starks.'

In the drawing room, Robeson enquired kindly how she was. His was a difficult task; he was prepared to make all the appropriate noises of sympathy, glad he had Mary's sensitive backing. His anxiety was unnecessary. Helena Bray was not sedated as she had been last Saturday – she was awake, in command of herself, and obviously not given to self-pity.

'Thank you, officer, for everything. For everything that you and your men are trying to do. You're very kind, coming to talk.'

He felt inadequate, at a loss, by her thanking them. He had not found anyone yet with the slightest motive for killing her sister. He enquired kindly, 'Is Julie still with you? And the little boy?'

'My husband insists. It's quite unnecessary, but I suppose he's being kind. Perhaps he thinks there's still someone lurking out there.'

Robeson noted the small smile didn't reach her eyes.

'But I've got friends, 'specially in Social Services. They've brought wonderful messages. Lots from old people.' She smiled: 'I deliver meals on wheels. I hope to again, soon. People have been so kind.'

Robeson felt his faith in human nature restored. Yet to agree that work, and thinking of others, would help her, might sound trite. 'Mrs Bray,' he asked gently, 'have you noticed any strangers lately? Anyone at all, perhaps walking, or in a car?'

'Yes, I do remember seeing a car last week. The driver kept looking in the drive. My husband will insist on keeping the gates wide open during the day.'

'Do you mean he stopped so he could keep on looking?'

'No, he crawled by several times, I mean different days. I thought perhaps he was admiring the camellias. People do.'

'Did you see what he looked like?'

144

'I didn't see his face. I believe it was half hidden. He kept backing, then he'd brake at the entrance, and look in.'

'Do you know what sort of car?'

'Yes, at least I think so. I believe . . . I can't be sure. It could have been a Mondeo.'

'Can you remember what colour it was?'

'It was green, like mine.'

Robeson paused a moment, and nodded before saying casually, 'May Inspector Starks and I take a stroll around your grounds, Mrs Bray? Would you mind?' He knew that if he wanted to, he would in any case, but this woman deserved courtesy.

'Please do. Whatever you wish. You won't mind if I don't come?'

They left by the front door. Going down the steps, they were first attracted by the camellias bordering the left of the drive. Bushy shrubs loaded with white blooms, and others with red, continued around the side of the house.

They strolled towards them. Robeson led the way through a gap, and stopped in the path that ran along behind. It was carpeted with needles from the overhanging pines: 'See, Mary,' he said, turning his head in the direction of the road, 'there's the little gate you saw from outside on Monday.'

'You mean, marked "Tradesmen"?'

'We could follow this path from it, and get up around the links, but . . .'

'What sir?'

'Waste of time. It's been brush-combed, and so have the links. Nothing.'

'Why did you ask Mrs Bray then, sir? Just because it's a nice morning?'

He grinned. Mary Starks was too astute to think that. 'Because as the gunman left no trace, we can forget which way he came, and concentrate on the position he came to.'

'Where do you think, sir?'

'I don't think, Mary. I deduce. That gun was fired from about ten yards. Ballistics have the bullet, and they know exactly.'

'You mean it was fired from about where we're standing?'

'You're getting warm, Mary. See, we're in a direct line from those steps.' He glanced all round about them. Behind, running alongside the path they were on, was a dense woodland of pine trees forming a natural partition between them and the golf links. Some trees had been brought down in the winter gales, and their sawn trunks were piled by the path inside the gate.

He sauntered up the path, and there being barely room for other than single file, Mary followed. Drawing level with the back of the house, he stopped as Ben appeared on a red tricycle and, as the child turned to pedal down the side of the house, Julie came running after him: 'No Ben, come back!' She and Ben stopped in their tracks on seeing the detectives on the other side of the bushes. The boy looked up wide-eyed, dangling one foot each side of the trike.

Robeson called cheerfully, 'Hello. It's Julie, isn't it, and Ben?'

'Oh.'

'We're just looking around, luv. I've had a word with Mrs Bray.'

'Oh.'

'You needn't sound so nervous, luv. This is my colleague, Inspector Starks.'

Julie smiled. 'I was just stopping 'im because 'e mustn't play out the front.' She started to turn the trike with Ben still on it.

Robeson glanced at the boy who had kept his eyes on him. 'Well, how are you today, chubby cheeks?'

Ben hunched his shoulders and shuffled his feet.

'Not shy, are you? Remember me, don't you?' Robeson squeezed through a gap in the bushes to stand beside him.

'No . . . oo.'

'Yes you do, Ben,' Julie said. 'The nice man what come in the kitchen on Saturdee.'

Ben gave a wicked grin. He remembered all right, and he proved it by saying, 'I got a hanky.'

Robeson grinned. 'I know. You showed me. Well, a little bit.'

' 'tis'n' yours.'

'No. 'Course not.'

'Mine.'

Robeson indicated Mary. 'Tell the lady.'

Ben scrutinised Mary with open curiosity, then glanced at Julie before turning back to tell Mary, 'I got a hanky. It's mine. Not no one else's.'

Mary bent her knees and crouched down so that her face was on a level with his: 'That's nice. Are you going to show me?'

He shook his head. 'No . . . oo.'

'It's indoors somewhere, or at home.' Julie looked at Robeson. 'He puts it down now sometimes, and leaves it.'

Ben said, 'Aaa . . . for Anna . . . leese.'

'Ah. That's nice,' Mary assured him.

Robeson liked Mary's way with kids. She would have been married with some of her own by now, if her boyfriend had not been killed in Ireland. It was a bloody shame.

'And who gave you the hanky, Ben?'

His round eyes looked into Mary's. 'It growed.'

'He picked it up,' Julie explained.

Ben rounded on her. 'It growed! On a tree!'

'All right, Ben. I'm sorry.' She looked at the officers. 'I thought he'd picked it up, I s'ppose he means he found it on a bush, that's higher than him.'

147

Ben stamped his foot. 'It growed on a tree!' His plump face reddened and his lips quivered.

Mary's arms went around him. 'Of course it growed on a tree, didn't it, Ben?' She looked into the eyes near to tears. 'They don't know, do they? They're silly, aren't they?' She hugged him, and waited a moment, then whispered, 'Would you like to show me, just me, pet, where it growed?'

He blinked at her.

She took out her own clean white handkerchief and dabbed his eyes. Julie and Robeson looked on. Mary straightened up.

Slowly Ben pedalled towards the end of the bushes, onto the path which Robeson and Mary had just come along. He turned, and carried on down towards the little gate. Mary followed, with Robeson and Julie in single file a couple of yards behind.

The path was not too smooth for little wheels. Ben stopped to lift his trike over a bump of pine needles. He stopped a second time to clear aside some twigs.

Robeson wondered where he was leading them. Perhaps the artful little blighter wanted to go home.

Ben stopped about two yards from the gate. He got off the tricycle and ran up to the pile of tree trunks and put his little finger on the end of one, and turned to Mary. 'It growed there!' He sounded triumphant.

Mary went closer. The ring-patterned insides of the felled trees shone with globules that looked like dew: 'Thank you, Ben. And that's a tree, isn't it? It's not a bush.'

He hunched his shoulders and bared tiny teeth, obviously delighted to have been proved right.

She touched the wood, pulled a face, and withdrew her fingers to wipe them on her handkerchief.

'Come o . . . nnn' Ben whined, pulling her hand.

'Coming, pet, just a moment.' She glanced higher, above where Ben's hanky had growed, then turned back to Robeson waiting on the path. 'Anything here for your birds, sir? They'll be nesting soon, won't they?'

Ben tugged her skirt. 'Come o . . . nnn . . .'

Robeson joined her and peered closely to see what she meant.

Impatient, Ben straddled his tricycle and, with Julie in tow, pedalled away.

Robeson took tweezers from his pocket, and removed from the resin-sticky wood what appeared to be some red hairs. He placed them carefully in a small polythene bag, just as he did with all items that may be of interest for examination by forensic. As he labelled and sealed it, they exchanged glances, and Robeson grinned. It was amazing what could be so easily missed; or had the hairs been brought on a breeze, since this part of the grounds was scoured on Saturday and Sunday?

He let Mary go first back up the path. He plodded behind, asking himself questions; his mind, as Janet called it, a permanent quiz game. Was Ben's hanky in the least important? It may not even have been dropped on Annaliese's last walk, but lost ages ago and blown from somewhere else onto the tree trunk where Ben had found it? And reddish hairs? Had she leaned there? Nothing made sense. She did not shoot herself.

He shrugged. Hanky and hairs were probably a waste of time, but you never gave up – detection included the same exciting chances as a game of roulette.

He found the others in the back garden. Julie, slim and wraith-like in her functional flowered overall, obviously had very few chores to do. Mary was already fussing over Ben. Robeson reached in his trouser pocket, then held out a pound coin. 'Thank you very much, chubby cheeks, for showing us your tree. Do you like ice cream?'

Ben's eyes lit up. Taking the coin he hunched his shoulders and bared his little milk teeth.

'And thank you, Julie, for your time.' He knew he had not wasted any of hers, and he hoped not too much of his own. 'Now we'll just have another word or two with Mrs Bray before we go.'

There was not much more he could say to Mrs Bray for the moment. Whatever the outcome of this murder, he felt a little uncomfortable in her company, conscious of what was probably soon coming to her husband, which was bound to affect her. He wondered if she knew that the simplest kind of swindles often involved a syndicate of crooked professionals: a broker, an accountant, a solicitor, and sometimes an estate agent. But if she had any idea that her husband's flamboyant lifestyle, and his attendance at local functions as a person of respectability, might soon be coming to an end, she showed no sign.

He declined her polite offer of coffee for himself and Mary, and they left by the front door. From the foot of the flight of stone steps, he noted that beneath the drawing room that they had just left was a double garage with its up-and-over doors open. Inside was a green Mondeo. He glanced at Mary. 'Life's full of coincidence. I wonder how many of those reported cars belonged to Mrs Bray?'

Chapter 14

'About that green car, sir.'

'You sound pleased, Roger.' Robeson had barely arrived in the Incident Room after another press conference. Trust Sergeant Mills to get things going. 'So the driver's come forward?'

'No, sir. But a call from the small coachworks down on the quay. A fella took in a green Mondeo to be resprayed.'

'When? Within the past three days since our appeal?'

'Yes, sir. Same day.'

Robeson thrived on such brainless acts. 'So what colour car are we looking for now?'

'I don't know sir. The sprayer chap said he couldn't do the job. Not right away, like the fella wanted. He and his men are up to their eyeballs with work.'

'Lucky for some.'

'Aye, sir. But he reckons he'd go bankrupt if it wasn't for bad drivers, and insurance work.'

'So is the owner of the Mondeo going to bring it back later?'

'Apparently not. He went away with a flea in his ear. Said he'd get it done elsewhere.'

'Then, Roger, look up all the coachworks, car bodyworks, and whatever else they call them.'

'I have already, sir, but no joy, there aren't that many around here. No wonder they all seem busy. No one else seems to have been asked to respray a Mondeo. Least, not this week.'

'Well the chap who rang you, he must have seen what the man looked like.'

'He can't remember. The car looked in reasonably good nick to him. Not urgent. But he was busy, and didn't attach much importance, till he heard our appeal.'

'We'll send two DCs along. Get him to rack his brains. What about employees? Might be someone who noticed.' Robeson retired to his own office. It was the same old story. Somewhere in a shed, a lock-up garage, or even some remote corner of a field, there was a man painting his car. It astonished him that after the police notice went out, anyone would take a sought-after car for a professional respray. How naive could anyone get? And yet it seemed in spite of such blatant foolishness, because the coachworks had been too busy, the bloody man had still got away.

Robeson drummed his fingers on his desk with frustration. The phone rang and he grabbed the receiver, offsetting his tension. 'CID.'

'Sir.' It was Sergeant Mills. 'We've had a tip-off. A guy with an accent rang, saying he knows someone who drives a green Mondeo.'

Robeson groaned. 'Jesus Christ, what's new? Thousands of the bloody things have been seen this past hell of a week. Who reported this one?'

'He rang off without saying, but he gave us the name of the driver.'

'He did?'

'And we've looked up files, sir. The man's on record. He's got form. Three convictions for theft when he was eighteen.'

Robeson's adrenalin rose. He got up smartly. 'I'll be down, Roger.' It was the best news he had had after being in a fog for seven days, and groping for anything that looked like a lead. Yet what had petty burglary to do with shooting? What motive would such a man have had for killing Annaliese Meade? He did not intend to crush Mill's enthusiasm; it was, after all, their duty to grab every piece of a jigsaw, however unlikely, and hope it might fit in somewhere, or perhaps sometime.

In the Incident Room, he took a file from Mills and glanced at the address he had scribbled down. 'So, Roger, any ideas?'

'Easy enough to check, sir. It's a flat in Hartop road, just off the High Street.'

Robeson grunted. 'Where do they park their cars?'

'I can't say for all, but I've seen some parked outside.'

Robeson tapped the folder and handed it back. 'I've got these records upstairs. And some. Maybe something on computer. Thanks. I'll take a dekko.'

Upstairs, Robeson did some homework, and with the help of research done by a couple of the suspects team, he briefed himself on the past misdemeanours of a certain Joseph William Harris, now aged thirty. He had changed his address several times during the past ten years, but the records appeared to be up-to-date. It did not take Robeson long on the phone to get the go-aheads he needed, and learn from contacts that Harris lived at 6A Hartop Road with a hairdresser called Neville Acland.

Some hours later Robeson returned to the Incident Room and caught Sergeant Mills just going home: 'Your latest Mondeo driver, Roger. Joshua William Harris. You and I will go and check him out.' He was heartened that Mills did not pull a face at this last-minute job; it made life easier to be working with a stable, happily married man who was, at the same time, ambitious to get on.

'Right, sir. I'll just give the wife a bell; she wasn't expecting me to be late.'

Robeson glanced to the back of the room where Detective Constable Searle, also about to leave after a long day, was shutting down his newly acquired computer: 'And I'd like you to come, too, Mike. We'll have an eyeball at this flat. You and Roger can turn it over if need be.'

'What're we looking for, sir?'

'A gun, Mike.' Robeson moved towards the door, and the men followed.

'What kind, sir?' Mills asked.

'We'll know, Roger, if we find it. The ballistic boys are cagey, and quite right. Let press or public hear we want a man with a certain gun, and that's what we'll get. We want *them* to tell *us*.'

'I've checked the register, sir, and this man's got no firearms cert.'

'That means nothing, you know that.'

'How d'you feel about this Harris?'

'Strong, I'd say, if he's got a gun.'

'What motive, sir?'

'Christ knows. I can't see one and I know what you're thinking. But in this case, it seems we'll have to reverse my rule, and find the bugger who shot that girl first, and the motive after.'

They left the Incident Room to a handful of detectives who were already taking bets that Joshua William Harris, unemployed, was their man, or at least in the frame. He had got previous convictions. He had hair like straw that grew up from his head as if in permanent fright. And he drove a green Mondeo that, since the police appeal went out, he was apparently eager to have resprayed.

It was 7.15. But the March evening was still light; a good time, Robeson felt, to catch Mr Harris at home. He was on record as being quick to scarper if he thought it necessary. Ex-Borstal, attempted burglary, an unproved hit-and-run, and several times detained on suspicion for being in the vicinity of cars that had been broken into. But in spite of a list of past offences, he seemed for some time now to have gone straight. Either straight, or he had grown more clever.

Robeson did not intend to make their arrival obvious by parking outside where Harris lived, even if he could find a space not on double lines. With prior permission he drove into an insurance company's private park behind their offices just off the city High Street, a block away from Hartop Road.

The three detectives broke company. As strangers, they sauntered into the pedestrianised world of department stores, supermarkets, video shops and high fashion. Then each officer in his own time casually turned left into Hartop Road.

They knew the area; featureless three-storey brick buildings on each side, with small shops at ground level that were mostly patronised out of hours when the locals could not get further afield. During the day, despite by-laws, displays of fish, vegetables and junk trespassed onto the narrow pavement.

Above the shops, most of the symmetrical tall windows followed a trend for lace curtains that looked as if someone had taken a large bite from the bottom, or they had gone wrong in the wash.

The entrance to Harris's flat was up a dark alley between a window packed with knitting wool, and a barber's that boasted 'No appointment needed'. In the gloom, the detectives converged at a door marked '1 to 8 Hartop Road'. There was no bell, and Robeson tried the door. It opened, facing a flight of stairs almost too narrow for Robeson's girth. They went up as quietly as possible on the bare treads. Flats 1 and 2 were on the first landing, which smelt of cooking, and the ammonia of unwashed nappies dried around a fire. Two flights up, number 6A had a light oak door with a frosted-glass skylight, and a white bell push. Robeson pressed it.

The door was opened by a tallish man, aged about thirty, wearing faded jeans and a white singlet. 'What do you want?'

'Mr Joshua William Harris?'

'What d'you want?'

Robeson flashed his card. 'Detective Chief Inspector Robeson, CID. Detective Sergeant Mills, Detective Constable Searle.'

'Fucking Bill?'

'Aye, Mr Harris. Mind if we come in?'

Robeson knew they were as welcome as snow in summer; but on the landing below another door had already opened, heralding the presence of a nosey parker peering up the open banisters, and they were admitted with unceremonious speed.

The air in the flat was as if the lace-curtained window was never opened; it reeked of tobacco, sweat, perfume, and a reminder of baked beans in tomato sauce. The pink-papered walls, an obvious DIY job, wrinkled and full of bubbles, clashed with the faded yellow moquette of a sagging three-piece suite that filled the room.

'What d'you want?' Harris repeated. 'I haven't done nothing.' He stood facing them, hands on hips, obviously proud to display his muscular arms and chest, covered in hair that matched the colour of the corn-like stubble on his head.

'Just a few questions, Mr Harris.'

'Needs three of you, does it?'

'Just routine for the moment, Mr Harris.'

'Ratepayers' money, that's what it bloody well is. I haven't done nothing. Better sit. This is my mate, Nev, if it's any of your damn business.'

Neville pushed what he had been reading down the side of his chair. It looked like a woman's magazine. 'Good evening, officers.'

Robeson nodded acknowledgement of the high voice, and sat down on the sofa with Mills and Searle.

Harris slumped on the other chair. His posture seemed to proclaim an insolence.

In spite of that, Robeson noted that Harris crossed and uncrossed his jean-clad legs, then pressed his knees together as if his bladder had filled and any minute he would want to speed to the loo. His behaviour was at odds with his obviously desired macho image; the hairy shoulders, the sallow complexion inclined to spots and in need of a shave; and the double bass voice, a stark contrast to his mate's treble sing-song.

'Mr Harris, where were you last Saturday?'

'I haven't done nothing, I tell you.'

'Where were you last Saturday?'

'Here with Nev.'

'All day? What did you do?'

'I didn't do nothing.'

'Well you must have done something. Got up, gone shopping, or for a walk. What did you do?'

'I don't know, do I? That's a bloody week ago.'

'What did you do, say, in the morning? That shouldn't be too hard to remember.'

'I don't have to tell you nothing if I don't want to. I know my rights.'

Robeson noted young Searle had caught Neville's attention. With a coy smile and his head to one side, Neville was making sure the pink socks that matched his shirt, were noticed when he tweaked up his slim-fitting trousers.

Robeson said, 'Well, Mr Harris, what did you do last Saturday morning, say, after you got up and . . . ?' He had been going to say 'and shaved', but thought that might sound like casting aspersions. He changed it to, 'after you got up and did whatever it is you usually do on Saturday mornings?'

'I can't see it's any of your damn business.' He glanced at Neville, who was holding a packet of cigarettes out towards the constable.

Neville asked Searle, 'Would you like a puff?'

Searle cleared his throat. 'Thank you, no. I don't. Thanks all the same.'

Harris glared from one to the other, then glanced back at Robeson. 'I remember now what I done on Saturday. I went down to Drayford, didn't I? Other side of Draymouth.'

'Of course you did, Josh,' Neville said, oblivious to the dirty look he had been given a moment ago, and fixing a fresh cigarette into a long black holder. 'I remember, I said to you, you're going to Drayford today, didn't I, Josh?'

Robeson put no store by the corroboration. 'Did you have any special reason for going there, Mr Harris?'

'I went to the Boys Club, didn't I?'

Robeson waited.

Harris puffed out his chest. 'Teaching 'em to box, aren't I?'

'I don't know. It sounds interesting. Tell me.'

Harris recrossed his legs.

Robeson thought he read signs of agitation, something to hide, yet was surprised – Harris sounded more confident, as if he had found a let-out.

'This mate I had long time ago at school, we often had a bout an' got on champion. I met 'im in a pub, back along, an' 'e remembered me. He asked if I'd like to help with his boys down Drayford.'

'What's your mate's name?'

'Duggie Smith.'

'Where does he live?'

'Down Drayford, where else? If you don't believe me, ask their new bloody curate, the Club was 'is idea.'

'Did you drive down?'

'No buses.'

'You have a car?'

Harris shifted his legs.

Robeson did not wait for an answer. 'What sort of car have you?'

'An Austin, but I can't see what damn business it is of yours.'

'Come, Mr Harris, what sort, is it a Mini, or a Rover, or what?'

'I don't remember the fancy names they use. Like . . . Mayflower, and . . . It's an Austin.'

Robeson knew that while he grilled Harris, Mills and Searle would watch Neville, and register every flick of an eyelash, every facial muscle that twitched. He asked, 'Is it a Mondeo?'

Harris stood up and shook his sweaty shoulders as if loosening up for a fight. 'Could be.'

'Is it, or not?'

Harris faced the draped window, his back to the men. It did not hide his truculence: 'Maybe 'tis and maybe 'tisn't. None of your business because I haven't done nothing.'

'What colour is it?'

'Black.'

'In good nick?'

'Very. I look after it, don't I?'

'Where do you keep it? In the street?'

'I rent a lock-up, don't I? I can't show you, because it's getting dark, and there's no light.'

'We do have torches in the Force.'

Harris swung round. 'You're a pain in the arse, you lot. All you do is make tea, and poke yer nose into people's business. What yer trying to do me for? I haven't done nothing.'

Robeson stood up, he felt more comfortable questioning

159

eye to eye than gazing up from a settee that sagged almost to the floor. 'Mr Harris, if your black car is in good nick, why did you take it to Jackson's for a respray?'

'You like black, don't you Josh?'

'Keep out, Nev.'

'Pardon me for breathing.'

Robeson asked: 'Had you heard we were looking for a green Mondeo?'

'No I never.'

'Do you know Links Road?'

Harris blew out his lips and began shaking his head.

'Do you know where the Golf Club is?'

Harris's eyes shifted. 'What would I want with golf?'

'You have been seen in Links Road several times lately,' Robeson said, as if Harris had actually been identified. 'Perhaps you didn't know the name of the road that leads to the golf course? What were you doing there?'

'Riding round, I expect.'

'Waste of petrol, isn't it? Just riding round, when you're on the dole?'

'Gotta do something.'

'Do you possess a gun, Mr Harris?'

'No I bloody don't.'

Robeson sensed the man's bottle was going. 'Do you know it's an offence to possess a firearm without a certificate?'

'I haven't got a gun.'

'Then you won't mind if we have an eyeball round?'

Mills and Searle were already on their feet, casing the room. There were no cupboards, nor any space left for furniture with drawers. Mills opened a door into an adjoining room, and Searle followed him in, with Neville close behind.

Robeson said, 'Mr Harris, did you know a young woman was shot and killed in Links Road?'

Harris clenched his big fists; the muscles of his bare arms

shone with sweat and rippled like a boa constrictor about to strike. 'Is he trying to pin it on me? The bastard! I'll get him!'

'Who?'

'See if I don't. He's scum!'

'Who?' Robeson repeated. Harris was losing his bottle.

'No one!'

'You called him scum.'

'You fucking pigs! Don't give no one a chance.' Harris flailed his arms aimlessly in the limited space. 'Just because I've been in a spot of trouble once or twice.'

A dozen times or more, thought Robeson: for stealing, threatening behaviour and malicious wounding. He watched Harris wipe the sweat from around his mouth with the back of his hand, seemingly ready to break. 'Mr Harris, the shooting in Links Road happened last Saturday around lunchtime. But you were in Drayford then, with the Boys Club?'

'I bloody was.'

'Then why should it worry you, my asking routine questions?'

Harris sneered, 'Routine? With poodles? Even nuns only come in twos.'

'What time did you get home, perhaps for a meal, after the Boys Club?'

'I can't remember. Four-ish.'

'With the Boys Club till then?'

'Had a ploughman's in The King's Arms, didn't I? I stayed drinking, an' had a game of darts.'

This could be checked, and Robeson had a gut feeling it was true. But why the aggression? Was it Harris's hardened defence against the law? Or did it imply guilt? He had no motive, and could not have killed Annaliese Meade, but had he some obscure connection?

Robeson scratched his head. 'You said just now that the

161

bastard's trying to pin it on you. Pin what? And who? You called him scum.'

'I'm not telling you lot. I don't have to. I know my rights. I didn't kill the girl, and if he says I did, I'll murder the lying bastard.'

Robeson soft-pedalled. 'Mr Harris, you have nothing to be afraid of if the account you've given me is true. Who's this bastard that's worrying you?'

'I'm not saying. I didn't kill her. I want a solicitor.'

'It seems you don't need one, Mr Harris; you were in Drayford at the time of the shooting, unless it's proved otherwise.'

'It's the bloody truth.'

'Do you know anyone who had a reason to kill her?'

'No.'

'What about this "scum" you mentioned?'

'I'm not saying nothing. I haven't done nothing, an' that's the bloody truth.'

The other detectives came in, Searle's shoulder bearing the caress of Neville's slim hand.

Mills grinned, and held out a gun. 'All we could find, sir. And a few bits of jewellery stashed at the back of a drawer that Mr Acland says are his own.'

'Presents, weren't they, Josh?'

Harris did not answer.

Robeson was not interested for the moment in possible petty pilfering. He took the gun, tossed and caught it. 'How many old ladies have you managed to frighten out of their pensions with this toy, Mr Harris?'

'God's Honour I haven't . . .'

'We'll leave God out of it. I'm concerned with your honour, not God's. Still up to the same old tricks?'

'I haven't done nothing!'

'Not murder, maybe. You've no form. What else do you do for money?'

'I never killed her. He's scum!'

'Who, Mr Harris?'

'I never done it. Why d'you keep on?'

'Because something stinks. Did this "scum" kill her?'

'I don't know, do I? But he's scum if he says I did – I wasn't there.'

'And you won't tell me who he is?'

'I don't even bloody know, do I? It's a mystery to me, same as you.'

Robeson sensed a certain amount of truth; he felt he could leave and, if need be, come back later. For the moment he had no sound reason to take Harris to the nick. He glanced from one to the other, and said affably, 'Well, we'll leave you two in peace. Thank you for your time, you've been very helpful.'

They filed out and down the narrow stairs. It was not until they reached the High Street, and they each took a lung full of fresh air, that Mills spoke.

'What d'you make of him, sir?'

'He didn't do it. He might know who did. He might be paid to keep quiet.'

'Or be bumped off himself, sir?'

Robeson grunted. 'Anything's possible. I'll put him under surveillance, and get the research team to find out who he knows, who he sees, anything not already on file.'

'You really think there's a connection, sir?'

'I don't know. But every so often, I get a whiff of bad drains.'

Chapter 15

It would have been reasonable to have grilled Joshua Harris until he had coughed his guts. Instead, Robeson had decided it might be more fruitful to let Harris breathe again for the time being while, in the interim, CID officers worked flat out researching the suspects, and DCs, some emulating scruffs in jeans and trainers, mingled in clubs, bars and cafés. They were there, with ears flapping, to find out who knew who? Which unlikely people had contact? Who cohabited with whom?

Robeson had preferred this method; he did not want Harris silenced with a bullet – if 'scum' feared being grassed, he might even then skip the net.

The homework paid off. It was the usual story; the more you stirred the pond, the more muck came up, and tips poured in. Avidly Robeson gathered the tangle of bits, bobs and strands, relishing the challenge to unravel the knots. Until now, investigations into the shooting over a week ago of Annaliese Meade, had reached stalemate.

He ticked off on his fingers the most important jobs, debating at the same time in which order to interview suspects. Neville Acland was too close to Harris, and better left for the moment. And if, as Harris had implied, 'scum' was really in the frame, Robeson did not want him scared off. He reached for the phone on his desk, knocking over Janet's photo in his enthusiasm to dial the estate agent's, and ask Mr Price to come to the station, please, to have a word. This time he would have to lean on Price.

It was a good hour later when Ian Price arrived, blaming the traffic, stupid drivers, and pressures of business. I know, thought Robeson, blame something. Anything. He wondered, watching the pale face which would have been devilishly handsome even without the neat moustache and rakish sideburns, if Price had used the time to fix anything; to put any extraneous business to rights.

Genially, Robeson said, 'Take a seat, Mr Price, I expect you're wondering . . .'

'Just how can I help you this time, officer?'

Robeson could not see Price's legs under the table to know if they were crossed, or nervously twisted at the ankles. He was only aware of long, well-groomed fingers playing cat's cradle, and an intensity in Price's wide grey eyes.

'Just one or two things. And to recap on what you told me on Monday, the twenty-fifth.' He glanced at his notes. 'You said that on Saturday, the twenty-third, you took a Miss Roberts to St Mark's Church in Links Road.'

'That's right.'

'You said, about eleven o'clock.'

'That's right.'

'Are you quite sure it wasn't about ten-thirty?'

Price hesitated, and pinched his chin. 'No, I can't be sure it wasn't.'

'Hadn't Miss Roberts said what time she wanted you to pick her up?'

'I can't remember now. I suppose she must have thought I knew near enough what time. She didn't say when I picked her up, if I was too early, or late.'

'You said her mother waved to you from the window?'

'That's right.'

'And after you dropped Miss Roberts, at either ten-thirty,

165

or eleven o'clock, you went home because you had plenty to do, having lost your wife a month ago.'

'Correct.'

'Then, although Miss Roberts had said she would make her own way home, because she didn't know how long she would be at the church, you went out again at around twelve-thirty, and up to The Firs to see Mrs Bray?'

Price did not answer.

Robeson looked up from his file, and cocked an eyebrow.

Price sighed. 'Correct. Is all this necessary?'

'You were going to give her a cassette of Mozart Horn Concertos, and changed your mind when you saw Mr Bray's car in the drive.' He waited, then looked up and made eye contact.

'Correct again.'

Robeson heard the impatience, but he had already been about to change gear: 'Mr Price, do you know a Mr Acland?'

Price shook his head. 'Can't say I do.'

'He's a hairdresser. Gaunt. With deep-set eyes, and long-ish hair.'

Price paused, a finger on his chin. 'I met someone like that. On one occasion. Is he called Neville?'

'Where did you meet him?'

'What is this, officer?'

'Where did you meet him?' Robeson repeated.

'I went to dinner one evening with Mr and Mrs Bray, and he was there.'

'When was this?'

'There was a dreadful gale blowing . . . I lost four ridge tiles . . . it was the night before my wife . . .' He paused. 'The men were working on my roof next morning, when my wife slipped, and fell top to bottom of the concrete steps at the side of our house.'

Robeson nodded, and looked sympathetic. He referred

to his notes. 'Was that particular storm on the evening of the twenty-fourth of February?'

Price hesitated: 'Yes, it would have been . . . my wife . . . on the twenty-fifth.'

'Are you still friendly with Mr Acland? I mean since you met him that evening?'

'I haven't seen him since.'

'How did he strike you? Did you like him?'

'He was all right, I suppose. Not really my type.'

'Who's his type?'

Price shrugged, and gave a twisted grin. 'Certainly not me.'

That was easy to believe; Price without doubt would be a ladies' man. 'So he's a friend of the Bray's?'

'I presume so. He must be, if he was there to dinner.'

'But you said you were there, not so much as a friend, but because you occasionally do business with Bray. Am I right? D'you think Bray does business with Acland?'

'I don't know. Acland's a hairdresser.'

'P'raps he cuts Bray's hair,' Robeson said facetiously, and at the same time an idea struck him. His own unruly mop needed taming; perhaps he could make time to try Acland. 'Have they anything in common?'

Price shrugged. 'It sounded, from conversation over dinner, that Acland once ruined someone's hair, and Bray had defended him against her claims for damages.'

'Once?'

'Some years ago.'

'And he and Acland had been friends ever since?'

'Presumably. I don't know, and I can't say I care, for that matter. I don't entertain my barber.'

'No. Nor do many of us. But you do a lot of entertaining, don't you?'

'How d'you mean?'

'Don't you play the violin?'

'Oh, that.'

'And you're not a mean tenor?'

Price shrugged. 'That's not for me to say.'

'Are you always so modest?'

Price shrugged again.

Robeson regarded him shrewdly. 'Wouldn't you call yourself a man of many talents?'

'That would be presumptuous.'

'But you play golf, and squash?'

'I enjoy most sports when I've time.'

Robeson could believe that, noting Price's fine physique. 'How many clubs do you belong to?'

Price started to count on his fingers. 'The Sports Club, the Golf Club . . . a music club, book club, and the Conservative Club.'

Robeson was in no mood for flippancy; Price was in no position to be facetious. 'How about the Gun Club?'

Price started. He hesitated before saying, 'Yes. I used to belong to one of those, too.'

Robeson knew he had sprung a surprise. 'What happened?'

'When I came here, I hadn't the time: I'd bought a business. Shooting's not like riding a bike, you have to keep at it.'

'Do you still have a gun?'

'No, I haven't.'

'Do you still have a firearm certificate?'

Price raised his voice a little, 'No, I do not, because I don't own a gun.'

Robeson knew he would hear more if he said nothing, and Price mistook that for doubt.

'When I sold my gun, the number and all relevant details went into the records. You can check the transaction easily enough, it's all there.' He glared at Robeson. 'Just what are

168

you trying to imply, officer? I don't like the line you're taking with me one little bit.'

Robeson saw he was ruffled. 'Weren't you also an excellent rifle shot at Bisley?'

'Officer, what has that got to do with you?'

'I'm trying to get some daylight on a senseless murder.'

'But what has that got to do with me? It's ludicrous. You've gone off your nut!' He clasped his hands together, clenching his entwined fingers.

Robeson changed tack. He'd seen the moisture on Price's cheeks. 'Mr Price, how much business do you do with Mr Bray?'

'Surely, officer, business is confidential.'

'I just wondered. It's not important.' He hoped to put Price off-guard by making his remark sound like an aside. 'I just wondered if, as a friend, you did any business outside the usual run of things between solicitor and estate agent?'

Price shook his head, then said grudgingly, 'He has sounded me occasionally about projects that I've advised him against.'

Robeson assumed only mild interest. 'What sort of projects?'

Price shrugged. 'Like putting money into certain building schemes that I didn't think were sound.'

Robeson kept casual. 'Did he take your advice?'

'I don't know. He said no more about them.'

Robeson played five-finger exercises on the file in front of him. He had no reason to detain Price. He stood up, indicating the interview was over. From its dross, he had gleaned a nugget worth more than the time it had taken – Laurence Bray had some connection with Neville Acland. 'Thank you for coming, Mr Price. You've been very helpful.'

*

169

Ian Price wanted to see no more desks that day; facing Inspector Robeson over his, had been enough. Anything would be better: a game of squash, a round of golf, or a swing with his scythe to tidy the wilderness in his orchard; at least that would stretch his limbs, and burn up some of the despair inside him – if only he could summon up the will to do any of those things. He drove to the Sports Club and, without glancing at the familiar faces at the tables, he made straight for the bar.

'Hello, stranger,' the barman welcomed. 'Your usual?'

Ian shook his head, rested himself on a stool, and leaned sideways on the counter. 'Something stronger.'

He received a hard look. 'Whisky?'

'Double.'

'How are things? We've missed you.'

'So so.' Ian took the glass that was slid towards him. He hated sympathy, but he had to get back into the swim of things sometime, and it was over a month now. He drank the whisky quickly. It burned his throat; he was not used to spirits. He caught the barman's eye, and ordered another. Carrying it, he made his way to the floor-to-ceiling windows that overlooked the indoor pool. Only a handful of swimmers were still in the bright blue water; the club closed at ten. He finished his drink, took his glass back to the counter and, amid a general hubbub, trod his way out through the tables without looking left or right.

In the car park, he reached for his keys, passed his hand wearily over his face, and put them back in his pocket. It would only take 15 minutes or so to walk home, and the air would do him good. A breeze had sprung up, but it was dry. A new moon hung in the clear sky, and one brilliant star seemed, as he walked, to keep straight ahead.

By the time he reached home, his head felt better. He would get used one day to coming back to nothing; Carol had not been much company, but at least she had been there, not just an empty darkness. He switched on the light. The cats, as usual, had put themselves to bed. He made some black coffee, and drank it in the living room as he slipped off his tie, and kicked off his shoes.

In the bathroom, he paused, and sniffed. Perhaps he imagined he could smell perfume.

Ten minutes later, in his bedroom, ready for sleep, he pulled back his duvet and sprang away as if he had been shot.

'My God!' He reached for his trousers, shouting, 'Get out! Get out of there at once!' He scrambled into some clothes without stopping to fasten them. 'Come on, get out of there, how dare you come here again!'

Now clothed, he glanced at Gail lying naked, her head on his pillow. 'Get out!' he demanded. At least she had not painted herself this time.

She smiled, and arched the small of her back to push out her tiny breasts with their pink nipples erect.

'Get up!'

She went on smiling, and held out her arms.

'Get up, get dressed and go home.' He realised he had left his car at the Sports Club, he couldn't take her. 'At once. I mean it.'

Her lips quivered. She moaned, 'I love you, Ian. I love you, I worship you.'

'Get up and go!'

'Please, Ian, love me.'

He kept his distance.

She pleaded, 'Please, Ian, I want you, I haven't seen you for three days, I can't live without you, I've tried.'

'Get up!'

She began to cry.

He threw the duvet to cover her until such time as she realised it was hopeless to stay. He crossed the room to stand by the window. He needed comfort, but not hers. For

171

three years he had respected her as the most competent member of his agency staff. Now she disgusted him. She was repulsive. He wanted only one woman, but Helena belonged to someone else.

Gail howled, 'I love you, Ian, I love you.'

He glanced back to see her throw off the duvet, arch her back and spread her legs. 'I'll kill myself if you won't love me, please love me, Ian.'

His head swam. He pinched his throat. Oh God, what shall I do? He felt like hurling her through the window, but forced himself to stay where he was, and appear calm. 'Gail, if you don't get up, and get dressed, and go home at once, I'm calling the police.' It was the last thing he wanted to do; he had had enough strain today from the Law, for whatever reason they had been ferreting out things about him. God knows what they would make of this.

He heard her snivelling. She moaned. He waited. At last there was some movement; she was getting up, still crying.

He remained motionless as she started to dress. He had once felt almost sorry for her. Now in his fury he looked at her, allowing himself to be critical for the first time. The beige tights; she had not even learnt the allure of a sheer black-stockinged leg.

She sniffed, 'I'll kill myself.'

He dare not tell her not to be a silly girl, he had made that mistake last time. He waited until she was fully dressed, with her coat on.

'You'll have to walk home the way you came. I haven't got my car.'

She sniffed, 'I'd do your washing.'

He saw a lace of saliva over her lips, she looked pathetic.

She whimpered, 'I'd darn your socks. I'd cook your breakfast, and look after the cats.'

Against his better nature he did not bother to thank her.

172

He thought, she's mad. Demented. Without a word he propelled her to the front door, opened it, and restrained himself from giving her a sharp push out before closing it sharply behind her.

Chapter 16

Robeson had plenty to chew on as he drove home after his interview with Ian Price. It was clear from what Price had said that Laurence Bray knew Neville Acland; in which case, Bray would most certainly also know Harris. But from what Robeson had seen, Harris would not be so acceptable, as Acland apparently had been, to sit at Bray's dinner table in the company of his wife, sister-in-law and Mr Price.

Robeson pondered. He often worked while still at the wheel; the road beyond the city towards his sleepy village needed less of his undivided attention. Was Bray the 'scum' that Harris had mentioned? Bray was the only person that Robeson knew of who had the slightest motive. Julie had said he hated his sister-in-law. Julie had overheard him say of his sister-in-law that he would be glad to be shot of her.

But Bray could not have killed her. Several motor mechanics, and some independent witnesses, had confirmed that Bray was at the city garage all Saturday morning. His car was immobilised until half past twelve, when he drove home. His sister-in-law was already dead.

Had Bray paid someone to do his dirty work? It could not have been Harris; he had been in Drayford nearly all day. That had been confirmed by the new curate, and by a young physical training teacher called Duggie Smith from Draymouth Comprehensive. And by several Drayford lads whom Harris, in his capacity of having been enlisted to help with the Boys Club, had shown how to side-step a left lead, and deliver a short right to their boxing opponent's body.

Was it Acland? He looked scarcely strong enough to wield a stick of forced rhubarb. Had Harris put on a star acting performance to protect him? But what motive would Acland have had? Unless money. Bray's money. And where was the gun? Mills and Searle had found none capable.

Cruising along the quiet road, Robeson tapped the steering wheel, and recapped. Bray had secured airline tickets for himself and his secretary. And however much he had wanted his sister-in-law out of his way, he had solved his problem by securing a place for her in a Residential Home. So why would he pay someone to kill her?

Robeson's nostrils filled with the stench of stale fish. He engaged bottom gear. Had the bullet, whoever fired it, been meant for Bray's wife? He turned into the open gateway of his rural semi-detached, and drove straight into the garage to leave the car – he hoped – for the night. Later, having tucked in to Janet's usual home-cooked beef casserole that had been ready and waiting for him, he mopped up the last of his gravy with a piece of bread, and glanced up.

'I guess you enjoyed that,' Janet smiled.

He had been miles away; had hardly noticed after the first satisfying mouthfuls. 'Delicious, luv. My favourite.'

'You haven't spoken six words since you've been in.'

'I'm sorry, luv. Dreaming.'

'You always are,' she teased good humouredly. 'It's lucky I know you. If I looked inside that curly head of yours, I reckon all I'd find would be a great big quiz game.'

He got up, and gave her a peck on the cheek. 'Thanks, luv.'

It was nice to have an evening together. He settled to relax in his favourite armchair, but he had already read the newspapers, and Janet's choice of television invariably sent him to sleep. It was not long before, against a background

175

of sit-com and canned laughter, and in spite of his resolve not to bring his work home, his mind strayed. Harris knew something. He definitely knew *something*. Then so must Acland. Perhaps he was not the harmless effeminate companion that he appeared. Tomorrow a DC would go along to the hairdressers' where Acland worked, and bring him to the Station. He would be leant on hard.

The third floor office at Headquarters emitted a fragrance of eau de cologne that was overpowering; certainly unusual for the workroom of anyone as masculine as Howard Robeson. He caught the eye of Sergeant Mills who, at the side of the room, was here to learn, observe, and take notes during this interrogation of Neville Acland.

Robeson's nose twitched.

In response, Mills gave a small sniff.

Robeson glanced at Acland. He had sat himself well back from the table, making it easy for his legs to be seen crossing and uncrossing, and then his knees pressed together to control his bladder. Robeson thought the bundle of nerves could do with a damn good meal; a bit of Janet's cooking. The pink, flowered shirt Acland was wearing appeared at least two sizes too big.

'Mr Acland, do you know Mr Bray, the solicitor?'

'Of course I do, I would, wouldn't I?' he simpered.

'Why would you? How did you first meet him, in what circumstances?'

'I went to him to help me, didn't I?'

'What kind of help?'

'There was this woman, wasn't there?'

'What woman?'

'She was going to sue me. I'd done her hair, I do tints. Some people call them colourants, but I prefer tints, it sounds nicer, don't you think?'

'What happened?'

'Her hair went green, so I went to Laurie.'

'Laurie?'

Acland giggled nervously. 'Mr Bray.'

'Was he Laurie to you then?'

'No. I'd never been to a solicitor before. Laurie, I mean Mr Bray, he found out that before she came to me, she had used something on her hair that she should not have used.'

'When was this?'

'Five . . . no, p'raps I tell a lie . . . six years ago.'

'And Mr Bray acted on your behalf?'

Acland clutched at a piece of silky brown hair that curled around his ears, and twirled it around his finger. 'I was ever so grateful.'

'But it was business. He was paid.'

'I had to have assistance, didn't I?'

'And just through his doing his job, you became friends?'

'I wrote to him, didn't I? I went to see him several times to thank him, I was so relieved, wasn't I?' He dabbed his high, pink cheekbones with a handkerchief from the pocket of his skin-tight trousers, and then flicked it, recharging the room with eau de cologne. 'If it hadn't been for Laurie, goodness knows what would have happened to my reputation. I'm creative, you see, aren't I?'

Robeson grunted. They seemed an odd pair; Bray, from reputation, was fond of women. 'Mr Acland, what do you do after work, in the evenings?'

'I'm fit for nothing, you'd never believe. By five o'clock, I'm right wrung out after standing all day.' He dabbed his cheeks again, pressing them as if to ensure their colour stayed put. 'My poor little old legs.'

'Mr Acland, what did you do on Saturday, March the twenty-third?'

'I always work till one.'

'And did you that day? Did you leave the premises at all?'

177

'How could I, Mr . . . Howard . . . ?'

'Officer will do.'

'Well how could I? I was doing a perm, wasn't I? You can't leave that, it's got to be timed just right, and . . .'

'Never mind the detail, what time did you *start* work?'

'Half past eight on Saturdays. Mario and Adrian, any of them, will tell you.'

'And were you there at half past eight?'

'Of course, I had Miss Thingummy's perm to do, didn't I?'

'And you didn't leave the premises at all until one o'clock?'

'No I didn't. Not with two perms and several manicures.'

'What did you do for the rest of the day? After you left work at one o'clock?'

'I put my poor feet up, that's for certain, I always do.'

'Were you alone in your flat?'

'Until Josh came home.'

'What time was that?'

'Dearie me, I can't remember, not to be precise.' He recrossed his legs. 'I'd say about four.'

'In the meantime, had you been to see anyone?'

'I told you, Mr . . . officer, I'm limp as a rag after work. I didn't go out.'

'Did you contact anyone?'

'How do you mean? How could I?'

'I didn't suppose by carrier pigeon. Did you telephone anyone?'

Acland hesitated. He reached for his handkerchief and pressed its eau de cologne to his forehead.

Robeson interpreted the gesture to mean yes. 'Who did you telephone?'

'I didn't telephone anyone,' Acland said with surprising conviction.

'I believe you did. Who was it?' Robeson had no idea that

he had phoned anyone, the accusation was one of his long shots.

'I did not. God's honour, I did not.'

Robeson changed gear; the pale blue eyes, staring across at his own, appeared more hollow, filled with fear. 'Mr Acland, you do admit you know Mr Bray?'

'Yes.'

'Well enough to go to his house to dinner?'

'I've only been once.' He sounded like someone trying to shake something nasty off of his foot.

'But you admit you know him well; you're on social terms?'

The orbs of colour on Acland's high cheek bones deepened. 'Yes.'

'Who shot his sister-in-law?'

Acland jumped. His hand flew to his mouth to gnaw his finger nails.

'Who shot her?' Robeson repeated with the sudden force of banging home a nail.

Acland stared over his fist.

Robeson leaned quickly towards him as though he were suddenly angry, suddenly frustrated by not getting information which he felt was so near to the surface but, like a fish, could swim beyond reach if he was not as quick. 'Who shot her?'

There was a moment's pause. 'It wasn't Josh.'

'Why did you say that?'

Acland gnawed his nails.

'Did I say it was Mr Harris?'

Acland shook his head.

'Mr Acland, this was a particularly vicious, cowardly murder. I'll ask you once again. Who shot Mr Bray's sister-in-law?'

Acland began to cry. He pulled out his handkerchief and buried his face in the eau de cologne. 'I don't know.'

179

'Can I suggest you do know, and you won't say?'

'I don't know. God's honour I don't.'

Robeson waited. He wanted a result. It was here some-where. Let the man blab. It could not have been him, nor Harris, but there was something fishy; he would bet his next year's salary they were in the frame.

'Mr Acland, it's been established that neither you nor Mr Harris were in the vicinity of the scene of the crime when it was committed. When did you hear about it?'

'When he rang.' His hand flew to his mouth.

'Who?' Robeson pounced like a cat on a mouse. 'Who? Who? Who rang?'

Acland blanched and swayed on his chair, and Mills went quickly to steady him.

'Fetch him a glass of water.' Robeson had seen it all before. The man was not going to faint, but his bottle was going. Someone else was being edged inexorably into the frame and Acland had not meant it to happen. Robeson waited while Acland sipped the water Mills brought.

Acland touched Mills's hand that held the glass; shaking too much to hold it himself. 'Thank you.' After a few sips he pushed the glass away, and looked up into Mills's eyes. 'You're very kind.' He took a small bottle of scent from the pocket of his flowered shirt, and dabbed his wrists.

Robeson tapped an impatient tattoo on the desk; he wanted a result, however long it might take having to listen to Acland's high sing-song. Assuming him ready, Robeson repeated the question that had had its unnerving effect: 'Mr Acland, who phoned you?'

'I didn't ring anyone.'

'Answer my question. Were you speaking the truth when you said you didn't telephone anyone on Saturday after-noon, the twenty-third of March?'

'That's the truth, God's honour.'

'But someone rang you?' Robeson watched the swallow-

180

ing movements of Acland's prominent Adam's apple: 'Who was it?' The only sound in the room was Mills shifting his notes. 'I can have the call traced if you won't answer,' Robeson said, not sure he could, but hoping that under this threat, Acland would save him the bother.

'Josh didn't do it.'

Robeson raised his voice; it was unlike him, but this man knew something: 'Why do you keep saying that?'

Acland began to cry again, this time noisily into his handkerchief.

'Who phoned you?'

'No one. I can't remember.'

'You're lying. Do you want to stay here all night?'

Acland howled.

'Who was it?' Robeson shouted.

Acland sobbed, 'Mr Bray.'

Robeson had guessed it. 'What time was this?'

'I . . . I . . . can't remember.' Acland jerked between sobs. 'N . . . not to be precise.'

'Roughly will do.'

'It . . . it was . . . perhaps about half past six.'

Robeson waited for Acland to look up, to make eye contact, before he continued relentlessly, 'Mr Bray's sister-in-law had been murdered earlier that same day. What was so urgent that he had to contact you?' He waited while Acland sniffed and dabbed his eyes, then raised his voice again. 'What was so urgent?'

Acland twisted his legs around each other.

'Think back! What did Bray say? It must have been pretty important that it couldn't wait.' Robeson fixed his gaze on Acland's pale, hollow eyes blinking back at him from across the table. 'After all, his sister-in-law had been murdered only a few hours earlier, the household was in a state of shock. Was he in a cheerful mood?'

Acland twisted his handkerchief around his finger. 'He

was angry, I didn't know what he was talking about, I said it wasn't Josh.'

'Let's take this more slowly. Why was he angry?'

'I didn't know, did I?'

'Why did you say it wasn't Josh?'

'Because it wasn't.'

'What wasn't Josh?' Acland did not reply. 'Did you mean it wasn't Josh who killed Miss Meade?'

'Yes.'

'Should it have been?'

'Josh didn't do it.'

Robeson contained his anger: 'Mr Acland, are we talking about conspiracy to murder? Do you want me to arrest you for withholding information?'

He saw Acland's thin shoulders slump forward, and guessed the weight of deceit was too much for him. His bottle had gone completely, and he was rowing for the shore.

'Laurie . . . Mr Bray said, "My God, you've made a bloody cock-up. You've killed the wrong bloody woman!"'

There was a seemingly long, silent pause before Robeson asked, 'Mr Acland, who were you supposed to kill?'

Terror filled the pale blue eyes: 'I wasn't going to kill anyone, God's honour I wasn't.'

'Was Mr Harris meant to kill someone?'

'He didn't!'

'Had it been arranged that he should?'

Acland blew his nose. 'Perhaps . . . there'd . . . there'd be an accident . . . with the car.'

'And who was to be his victim?'

Acland snivelled, but didn't answer.

'Was it Mrs Bray? Mr Acland. Answer me. Was it Mr Bray's intention that his wife should be killed?'

Acland sniffed as he nodded.

Robeson and Mills exchanged glances. Robeson looked

back at the thin man slumped on the opposite chair. 'I presume Mr Bray was going to pay you handsomely for killing his wife?'

'We didn't,' the high squeaky voice protested.

'Your conspiracy to do so will be dealt with later. For now, who *did* kill Bray's sister-in-law?' He glared, awaiting an answer.

Acland bent his head and covered his eyes with his hands: 'I don't know, God's honour, that's the truth, I don't know.'

Robeson shot a helpless glance at Mills. As far as finding who murdered Annaliese Meade, Robeson felt he might as well be playing a game of Snakes and Ladders. After all his interrogation, instead of making progress, he had arrived on the snake's head, forced to slip back down to its tail, and start again.

Chapter 17

Things looked black. Robeson had not digressed to deal personally with Laurence Bray's abortive conspiracy with Acland and Harris; it would be dealt with. And he had left Laurence Bray's come-uppance to the Fraud Squad. He had concentrated his own enquiries on their main artery – the murder. But after four weeks, what had he got to show? Bugger all.

Janet soothed, 'Now, now. Have your breakfast.'

'Thanks, luv.'

'And here's the local paper.'

He glanced at the banner headlines beside his plate, and grinned; she had never cured him of reading at meal times. 'Crooked Lawyer's losing streak'. 'Well, that's one bugger at least, who'll be doing a nice long stretch for playing Monopoly with his clients' money – whatever else he might think he's got away with.'

'Why are you so cheerful?'

He reached for the mustard. 'Because I've nearly stepped on his tail myself, more than once, but he was always more slippery than a buttered eel.' Robeson did not usually discuss cases, but it was all here in black and white. 'Laurence Bray has speculated for years in dubious property deals, and gambled on the stock market. Too bad he had to dip into the estate of a dead man, and the accounts of other clients to cover his losses.'

Janet pulled a face.

'He got a nasty shock when the Serious Fraud Officers arrived with a warrant to search and examine documents. He was going to bunk off to Canada.'

'Your breakfast's getting cold.'

He picked up his knife and fork. 'It's his wife I'm sorry for. It seems that for some people it never rains but it pours.' He fell silent, and tucked into his eggs and bacon; he needed his daily fix of cholesterol to work on, and he did not want to discuss the murder of Mrs Bray's sister. He would be on that, by the look of things, until he was drawing his pension.

The murder hunt had settled into a predictable pattern; the first enthusiasms had waned, the first influx of phone calls had become a trickle. Even Superintendent Moore's briefings were stale, progress reports were a laugh, and the press had moved on to other things.

It was April now. Driving to work, Robeson's thoughts drifted from the hedgerows and trees that were bursting with fresh green, to the birds that would soon be building nests, laying eggs, sitting, then raising greedy families by dropping warm morsels into gaping gullets. It was the same the world over, he mused: house hunting, weddings, mating and babies; though in this age it seemed that mating and children came before the wedding.

He was reminded of St Mark's Church, and wedding bells. Mrs Bray had heard them on 23rd March. But she had not heard the gunshot that killed her sister, because she had closed her kitchen window to listen to Mozart on her cassette player. Had the murderer taken advantage of those bells to drown the sound of his gun? If so, who knew in advance at what time they would be peeling so loud and merrily? Who knew when Mrs Bray was likely to be at the back of the house?

Robeson stopped at the traffic lights. Who? he asked

himself again. Ian Price? He knew, because he had said he gave one of the bell ringers a lift to the church. He was infatuated with Mrs Bray, and knew her sister. The lights changed. He shook his head and drove on.

Long after the day's briefing, and ferreting among the lads in the Incident Room for anything new, thoughts of Ian Price persisted. But motive? Desiring Mrs Bray without the encumbrance of her sister could not be motive enough; he was not the type. Robeson corrected himself from being complacent; there was no special type, the most unlikely people committed murder.

He thumbed Price's statement. Price had known of Miss Meade's daily habit of walking around the links before lunch. And he had known exactly when the bells would be ringing; he said he had taken a Miss Gail Roberts, a bell ringer, to the church. She must be brought in for a word. He picked up the phone and gave instructions to a DC on the floor below.

Robeson faced Gail Roberts across the desk. She seemed pleased; flattered by his every word.

'I came right away,' she said unnecessarily, since DC Searle had brought her by car. 'Mind if I smoke?'

Sergeant Mills got up, produced an ashtray from some-where, and pushed it within her reach.

'Ta.'

Robeson disliked smoking, but never refused a request; he saw it as an interviewee's prop to offset their nerves. He took stock of her while she made a great performance of lighting up. She was about forty, with a thin, pale face and dead straight hair worn with a fringe. It was as black as the toast Janet sometimes forgot was under the grill.

'Miss Roberts, it's just routine, but it might help us. Did you work at Price's, the estate agent's, until recently?'

'Yes.'

'How long were you there?'

'Three years.'

'When exactly did you leave?'

She paused to think. 'About three to four weeks ago.'

'Would that be about March the twenty-fifth?'

'That's right, about then.'

'That was the beginning of a week. How come you finished then?'

She pulled on her cigarette, then exhaled a curl of smoke that drifted lazily towards the ceiling. 'We had our differences.' She looked vulnerable in her drearily correct two-piece suit, set off with a heart-shaped brooch. 'He was getting very difficult.'

'In what way difficult? Worried? Bad-tempered? As if he had something on his mind, or what?'

'All of that, officer.' She tapped ash into the tray.

'Did he sometimes take you out?'

'Occasionally.'

'Did he take you to the Sports Club sometimes?'

'Yes, quite often; he liked to before he . . . sort of got moody.'

'Miss Roberts, did he drive you to St Mark's Church on Saturday, the twenty-third of March?'

She lit another cigarette, discarding most of the first. 'No.'

He showed no surprise at her extravagance, nor her answer: 'Are you quite sure about that?'

'Yes. Why? Did he say he did?'

'Miss Roberts, was there a wedding at St Mark's on Saturday, the twenty-third of March?'

'I believe there was.'

'Are you a bell ringer?'

'Yes.'

'How many bells are there at St Mark's?'

'Eight.'

'Are there spare ringers if someone doesn't turn up?'

'There are a couple who could step in, I suppose, if they were there. But it's quite possible to manage with only seven bells.' She tapped her cigarette. 'Ordinary people wouldn't hear the difference.'

Robeson grunted: 'Had you intended going?'

'Yes. I remember now. I had a migraine.'

Robeson frowned. 'Does Mr Price live a couple of hundred yards beyond where you do?'

'Yes.'

'Does he have to pass your house on his way to town, or go to the church, or to the golf links, or wherever?'

'Yes. Our road's a dead end.'

'Did you see Mr Price at all that morning?'

She drew on her cigarette, tapped off some ash, and exhaled through her nose.

Robeson prompted, 'Can you remember if he paused in your gateway as he passed? Perhaps because he had been going to give you a lift, but didn't know about your migraine?'

She still did not answer at once. He waited; she ought to know Price better than anyone.

'He went by for certain. Like always.'

'Do you mean early, to go to work?'

'He didn't go in on Saturdays. Least, not since his wife . . .'

'Did you?'

'I had that morning off.'

'For the wedding?'

'Yes, but then I had this migraine, and . . .'

'Did you let Mr Price know?'

'My mother would have.'

'Did she?'

'I don't know. I naturally presumed so.'

188

Robeson tapped his fingers on the file beside him. 'Did you, or your mother, see Mr Price drive past your house on the Saturday morning I'm talking about?'

'He did for certain.'

'Did you see him?'

'He would have.'

'What makes you so sure?'

She looked coyly at Robeson from under her straight black fringe: 'Perhaps I shouldn't say ... but why not? Going to the Brays I bet.'

Robeson turned on his charm, in the knowledge that Mills was taking notes. 'Please, Miss Roberts, tell me anything you know of Mr Price's whereabouts that morning. Why are you so sure he went to the Brays?'

'He's crazy about her, that's why. He was forever talking to her on the phone. Every morning. Sweet nothings. Disgusting. She a married woman, and his wife only dead two weeks.'

She crushed out her cigarette vigorously, splaying the unused tobacco over the ashtray. She fumbled in her bag, produced another, and lit it with shaking fingers as if the disgust of Price's behaviour still rankled.

Robeson asked, 'Do you know Mrs Bray?'

'No, and I don't want to.'

He guessed the words had slipped out. Inclining his head with a small smile, he hoped he appeared to understand.

'He used to moon over her fire-gold hair, her perfect figure, and her pert little nose. And she, a married woman!'

Robeson smiled: 'Well, Miss Roberts, you have been most helpful.' He glanced at Mills. 'Sergeant, show Miss Roberts down, and get someone to run her home.'

It had turned five o'clock when Robeson slipped behind the wheel of his car. Instead of making for home, he turned in the opposite direction and drove towards Links Road. Ten minutes later he pulled up outside St Mark's Church. He had no particular object in mind, except that he wanted to kill time before going back the road a little way, and then taking the turning which led to some fairly isolated bungalows. He wanted to give Ian Price time to have arrived home from his office.

In the churchyard, glimpses of confetti adhered to the gravel path. Little coloured heaps filled corners around the porch. Robeson went in and peered from the open church door into the gloom, and came out again.

'Hallo, guv!'

Robeson started. 'Hello, squire, what're you doing here?' he asked, recognising a local workman.'

'I could ask you the same, guv.'

Robeson grinned: 'I'm just killing time. Bob Smith, isn't it?'

'Aye, guv, just finishing me stint.'

'Do you work here now then?'

'Aye.'

Robeson had known the countryman by sight for years. 'Do you like it?'

'Aye. Not bad at all, considering. Clearing up and that, five full days, I don't come Saturdays.'

'So you miss all the pretty weddings.'

Bob chuckled. 'Aye. But I know when there's bin one, though.' He glanced round. 'Damn stuff sticks. But 'tis my church; I bin coming here every Sunday since I were knee-high to a cricket.'

'So you know everyone?'

'Aye.'

'The vicar, the choir, and the bell ringers?'

'Aye. All the lot. They'm a nice bunch. Mostly.'

'How many bells are there?'

'Eight. They'm lovely old bells.'

'Ever rung them yourself?'

'Aye. I 'ave an' all, when I were younger.'

'Who rings them now?'

'Ooo, let's see . . . there's two men, a couple of lads, and four ladies.'

'That's interesting; how would I get to know who these clever people are?'

'Ooo . . . I dunno. 'Tis practice tonight . . . or p'raps tis tomorrow, I ain't sure. So you like the sound of bells?'

'Mmm. I wouldn't mind meeting the sort of people who delight in tugging at ropes.'

'Well, if you'm that interested, there's a book in the church – it tells all about it. 'Tis alongside the visitors' book, and it tells 'e the 'istory, and names the ringers an' all that.'

'That's interesting.' Robeson watched the man put on some cycling clips. 'P'raps I'll have a peep directly. Is the church always left open? Some have to be locked these days.'

'Someone will be along soon. 'Tis choir practice, if 'tisn't the bells. I'd show 'e, but I'd better be off or the missus'll want to know what I've bin up to.'

Robeson strolled into the church. On a table beside the visitors' book, was a thick ledger, its hard green cover bearing an inch-wide faded border, as if there was usually something smaller kept on top. He opened it carefully. Inside, the ledger's early pages were freckled with age and smelt musty. Different handwritings down the years had recorded in varying shades of ink and legibility, the full names and addresses of members of the choir, and of the bell ringers of 'St Mark's of this Parish'. Beside some names, there were random jottings. He paid most attention to information relating to the more recent past: special occasions, potted biographies and scrawled riders. Using his regulation ballpoint, he made notes in his pocketbook and tucked it away inside his jacket.

He did not wait to see who of the church officials turned up. He got into his car, and before going to see Ian Price, he continued along Links Road. He would make a U-turn at the entrance to the golf links, then first of all he'd pop in to see Mrs Bray at The Firs. He had resolved to visit her tomorrow, to offer his sympathy and support, but he had changed his mind and wanted to see her now and, if possible, Julie.

The lime trees each side of the road displayed the lacy green of spring. It would outlast the beautiful, but short-lived pink flowers of the cherry trees that stood at intervals in between.

Parked outside the big iron gates of The Firs was Ian Price's cream Volvo. Robeson drove on to the entrance to the golf links, turned, then parked out of sight of The Firs while he decided what to do. Impatiently, he tapped the steering wheel. He wanted to see Price, but not with Mrs Bray. And he wanted to see Mrs Bray now. He fished for his pocketbook, perused his notes, and put them away. He drummed his fingers again on the steering wheel. He could phone her later this evening, but if she went out, he would miss her.

Ten minutes later, he heard the Volvo. It had been facing down the road, and if it hadn't taken a little trouble starting, he might not have heard it being driven off. He pondered how to approach Mrs Bray; he might be unwelcome, following so quickly on what was probably a tryst. As it turned out, his call was made easy; Helena Bray was at the far side of her drive cutting daffodils. As he opened the ornamental iron gate and went in, she straightened up, looking pale and sad, but every bit as pretty as before.

'Good evening, Mrs Bray.'

'Hello,' she smiled.

'I just wanted to say how terribly sorry . . .'

'Thank you, officer. That's very kind.'

He held out his hand to take hers. 'We're still working very hard, but if there is anything . . .'

'Thank you,' she smiled. 'But it's all right. I can cope.'

He held her hand firmly for a moment to reassure her his offer was genuine. 'Is Julie still with you?'

'No. There's nothing for her to do. I've given her a reference, she's a good cook.'

He nodded. 'Does she live far away?'

'About a mile from here, in Lymepark council houses. She used to cycle over. Had a seat on the back for Ben.'

He really wanted to know the number, but would not ask; he could soon find out – in Lymepark everyone would know everyone. He glanced admiringly at the wide border of daffodils. 'What a lovely show you have. And the trees. Everything's looking wonderful.'

She lifted her shoulders and dropped them with a heavy sigh. 'It'll all be going soon, I suppose.'

He locked his teeth together, he had said the wrong thing. 'Sorry, lass, try to bear up.'

'I will.' But in spite of her smile, and the proud tilt of her head, he saw the brown eyes had filled with unshed tears.

Leaving her, he debated whether to go and find Julie, or whether, if Ian Price had gone home, to go to see him first as he had originally planned. He drove on down Links Road. By the time he had left The Firs half a mile behind, and was on the city side of the church, he had made up his mind. He turned off into a narrow road which led only to fields and some isolated bungalows. It was little more than a lane, rough and rutted, having never been made up properly because of some dispute between property owners, builders and the local authority.

Avoiding a pothole, he drew alongside a small iron gate with a painted nameplate, 'Chambery'. The bungalow beyond it had a continental look; the main rooms and full-width balcony were built above the double garage. A staircase, with an iron balustrade that matched the wrought iron around the balcony, led up to the front door. He noticed that at the side of the split-level building, there were concrete steps, no doubt leading down from the kitchen, to a path which followed around and up a steep bank to an orchard at the back.

He climbed the front stairs and pressed a bell. Price opened the door almost immediately. He looked surprised, but not hostile.

'Mind if I come in? There are just one or two things I'd like reaffirmed.'

Price shrugged, and stood aside to make way.

Robeson avoided a row of saucers on the living room floor and, after being invited to do so, sat down in a rather shabby armchair.

'I've only just got in,' Price said. 'I was about to make tea. Will you have a cup?'

'Not just now, thanks, my good wife will be waiting with a nice cooked meal.' He stopped abruptly, he shouldn't have said that. 'I'm sorry.'

'You needn't be,' Price said.

'All the same, it was thoughtless.' Robeson rebuked himself; he usually chose his words so carefully, and that was the second time in half an hour he had slipped.

'What was it you wanted to know, officer?'

Robeson wondered what went on in that handsome head that appeared so calm. Perhaps it was love. 'I'd like to run over what you told me you did on the morning of Saturday, March the twenty-third.' He paused. 'What time did you go out?'

'I really can't remember. Not exactly. It may have been eleven o'clock, it could have been half past ten.'

'You said you called for a Miss Roberts, and took her to St Mark's Church in Links Road. Is that correct?'

'Yes.'

'Did her mother wave to you from the window?'

'Just what is this, officer?'

'Was that statement you made, correct?'

'Yes, but I want to know . . .'

'Does she live in a bungalow about two hundred yards down the road from here?'

'I told you so,' Price said shortly. He sat on a dining chair with his arms on a scratched oak table. A cat occupied each of the other three armchairs.

Robeson noticed several magazines on the table: *Guns Review, Gun 7 Accessories Mart, Clay Shooting*. He cocked an eyebrow: 'You're still interested in shooting?'

'Yes.' Price picked up a picture and handed it over: 'That's someone from my old club.'

Robeson read the caption aloud: 'Richard Smith shooting his Wilson-built Tasco-scoped 38 Super.' He looked at Price. 'So you still keep in touch?'

'He was my best mate.'

Robeson grunted and gave the magazine back. He paused a moment before reverting to business. 'Did this Miss Roberts say she was going to take part in ringing the church bells?'

'She must have, I suppose. Or I took it for granted.'

'Did you give her a lift to the church?'

'Yes.'

A proud, sulky-looking Persian with long, silky white hair strolled in. It paused at a saucer, and its flesh-coloured lips twitched; then a little pink tongue flicked out as it lapped the milk.

Robeson got up. He was surprised that the place, though clean, was so shabby – Price was acclaimed to be well-off. 'Well, thank you very much for your time, Mr Price.'

Price looked surprised. 'Is that all? Don't you want to know what I did next?'

Robeson ignored the sarcasm. Price had already told him

he came home to feed his cats, and had done odd jobs until half past twelve. Then he had gone to deliver a cassette to Mrs Bray. 'By the way,' he said as if it had only just occurred to him, 'did I see you leaving Mrs Bray's house just now?'

'You did.'

Their eyes met. Robeson cocked an eyebrow.

'I hoped I could give her a little comfort, officer. In that big house. With lonely rooms. And now this terrible news about her husband.'

Robeson nodded: 'She's a brave woman.'

Price stroked his sideburns, his eyes downcast. 'We all have our crosses, but hers have been blazoned across the press for the world to see.'

Robeson nodded again, and turned towards the door. 'Well, thanks for your time, Mr Price.'

He made his way down the iron staircase. He wondered if he could catch Inspector Starks before she went home: she might be useful to placate the little boy when he went to see Julie.

He was beginning to see a dot of light, but even now, at what he hoped was the eleventh hour, he could not be sure.

Chapter 18

The following morning promised hope. Despite a press conference which was difficult – because the media were getting impatient with the lack of information – Robeson tackled administrative duties and paperwork with renewed vigour. For weeks he had beavered away in vain for a result, and today he had a gut feeling his luck was about to change. Thanks to the research team, and the new CID computer system, he knew exactly were he was going; and why, and what for.

He went to the Incident Room to enlist the assistance of Inspector Starks. She had been wonderful with little Ben last evening when they had gone to Julie's council house, and he could rely on her to be just as invaluable now; prepared to accompany him to an interview, with everything organised as usual in her neat shoulder-bag. He caught her eye, and held up his hand.

'Yes, sir?' She came over.

'We're going to call on a Mrs Roberts, Inspector,' he said, using her rank in front of the men, not 'Mary', as she usually was when they were outside. 'I understand she's elderly, and disabled.' Together they went down the fire-proof stairs to the car park. He said, 'I'll drive. Her road is full of potholes. I was there yesterday when I went to see Ian Price.' He unlocked the car and climbed behind the wheel, leaving Mary to slide into the passenger seat.

The late-morning traffic had built up, and it was some time before Robeson was able to filter in. The drive that should have taken less than ten minutes, took twenty. After leaving the congestion, but before reaching St Mark's Church, he took a side road and continued up to its dead end. He turned the car, and on the way back, he slowed down to point out Price's place. About two hundred bumpy yards on, he stopped in a small bay in front of Mrs Roberts's garden gate. They got out and went in. Halfway up the crazy paving path they heard the sound of knocking; a woman was sitting at a front room window wielding a stick and gesticulating that they were to go in, the door was open.

In the small hallway was an oak stand hung with coats. They brushed by into the room where they were called. 'You must excuse my not getting up,' the voice continued with its perfect enunciation, 'It's my silly old hip, they've promised me a new one but goodness knows when.' The woman gave a theatrical laugh that almost shook the clutter of small ornaments and the framed photographs that filled every available space. 'I expect I'll be pushing up the daisies before it's my turn.'

Robeson smiled and flashed his card. 'Detective Chief Inspector Robeson, and this is my colleague, Inspector Mary Starks.'

'Yes, yes, of course, I've been expecting you,' she said, fluttering her long thin fingers as if she were playing the piano on her lap. 'There's coffee in the kitchen if you fancy it.'

Robeson refused quickly for both of them; if they wanted coffee it was obviously a case of do it yourself and he wanted to waste no time. 'Are you on your own?'

'My daughter's out looking for a job – so she says. Goodness knows why, she had a perfectly good one until a few weeks ago.' She tut-tutted. 'But that's her all over.'

He regarded Mrs Roberts thoughtfully; the hair dyed an unflattering red which clashed with her salmon-pink lipstick. 'Can you manage without her?'

'O my dear, perfectly; it's just the old hip. I can skipper the old bod around quite all right with my sticks, if I have to.' She pealed with laughter.

He contributed to her mood with a wide grin; she seemed a game old soul. 'What I've really come for, ma'am, is to ask you about your son, Charles Roberts. Has he been here recently?'

'Oh my dearh, of course. Now tell me, what's my darhling boy been up to?'

'How long was he here?'

'Not long enough, the naughty boy. And such a long way to come to see his poor old mother.'

Robeson inwardly agreed with the 'old'; the colour on her highly rouged cheeks only emphasised their deep lines. 'Where does he live?'

'Has he been a naughty boy?'

'Did he stay here?'

'Only for ten days. And after his poor mother had waited so long, and his coming so far.'

'Where does he live?' Robeson repeated.

'Natal, or South Africa, or whatever they call it these days. Do you know it, my dearh?'

'Only what I read,' he said, to save time.

'Do you know it my dearh?' she addressed Mary.

'It was in southern Africa when I was at school,' Mary said. 'But they've got a habit of renaming things, or moving them around since then.'

Mrs Roberts shrieked with laughter: 'Oh she's a card, just like myself. My dearh, I used to be just like you. I was very beautiful, the men used to flock round me, I expect you've got lots of boyfriends, too.'

Robeson admired Mary's nod and brave smile. He guessed she knew as well as he did that it was quickest to agree. He said: 'What does your son do, ma'am?'

'He farms. It's no place to be these days. I wish he'd come home like we did.'

'When was that?'

'Four years ago. D'you know, recently, a friend of my son's passed an African who greeted him politely, then said, "Sorry, boss," and stabbed a knife in his chest.'

Robeson frowned: 'What did your son do when he was here?'

'Mostly he stayed in with his poor old mother. My daughter was working then.'

'Where did she work?'

'I always hoped she'd be an actress, like I was. But of course, she never had the looks. I was very beautiful.'

'Where did she work, ma'am?' he repeated.

'Don't keep calling me ma'am, you make me feel old.' She patted her dyed red hair: 'She did work in the city, for Mr Price the estate agent, and I used to tease her about him no end.' She sighed. 'Such a handsome man, and plenty of money. I used to tell her she'd be a little fool not to hang her hat up there. And then when he lost his wife . . .'

Robeson waited to hear more. Mrs Roberts seemed excited to have an audience; her old voice was surprisingly rich and resonant as if she were still on stage. But with the green skirt she was wearing, and a blue blouse under a pink cardigan, she looked like a jumble sale in transit.

She went on: 'When he lost his wife, I really thought *bingo*, this was it. But no, what does Madam go and do? The little fool throws in her job.' She tut-tutted. 'Always boasting of her conquests, but I get no evidence. I say for goodness' sake bring your men home.' She paused, and looked grotesquely coy. 'To look at me you may not believe it, but she's over forty.' She waited as if for applause, or to give the officers time to express their amazement. In the ensuing silence, she went on, 'I tell her, you'll never get a man if you're a shrinking violet. Display yourself. Men, bless them, want to see what they're getting.' She pushed back her shoulders and thrust out her jumble sale breasts that, raised so high, obviously owed everything to an underwired bra. 'They want a promise of passion.' She laughed beyond what her comment justified. 'Isn't that so, officer?'

His small smile was non-committal as he watched her dab the mascara that ran down her cheeks. 'Did Mr Price take your daughter to St Mark's Church on Saturday morning, the twenty-third of March?'

'Oh yes, bless him,' she answered with no hesitation.

'Why are you so sure?'

'My son was here, and we both teased her not to keep lover-boy waiting.'

'And did she?'

'She seemed a long time putting on her face, so I waved to show him I knew he was there.'

Robeson nodded. It fitted.

She pursed her bright pink lips, pleating the skin around them: 'But she hasn't got what it takes, not the sex appeal I had, she's been a great disappointment to me.' She looked directly at Robeson. 'I really did hope that she and Mr Price . . . Not right away of course, so soon after his wife, that wouldn't have looked nice, but . . .' She reached down the side of her chair, then held a packet of cigarettes towards Mary. 'Do you?'

'Thanks, no, I don't.'

She moved them towards Robeson.

'No thanks, I don't either.'

She took one herself and produced a lighter from the pocket of her shapeless, pink cardigan. 'I'm just gasping for one,' she said, lighting up. She continued from where she had left off: 'I did hope she and Price. But the silly girl's got no idea. I tell her men are physical! And to do something about it.' Her face was veiled by the smoke from her cigarette. 'You men are physical, isn't that so, officer? Oh how I miss them flocking to my dressing room, those lovely physical men, and the grease paint, and the flowers, and all the applause.'

Robeson did not want to reminisce. 'Mrs Roberts, your son was here for ten days. When did he leave?'

'On Sunday, the day after Mr Price, bless him, had stopped outside.'

'Would that have been March the twenty-fourth?'

'That's right.'

'Did you know your son had a gun?'

She frowned, but did not seem put out by the question. 'My dearh man, what's the naughty boy been up to?'

'Did he have a gun?'

'I didn't see it, but it's quite likely. He had to travel through hostile country before coming over.' She fanned the smoke from her face. 'That part was bad enough before I left. We were all trained to shoot, and I believe it's worse now.' She drew on her cigarette, then exhaled: 'I wish the dearh boy would come home for good. I think several farming couples in the Natal midlands have been murdered.'

'Is he married?'

'No, the dearh boy's still footloose and fancy free. But it's different for men, isn't it?' She smiled at Mary: 'They can settle down when they've done with sowing their wild oats, can't they, deaarh?'

Robeson said, 'Does he live alone?'

'No. He's happy with a married couple on the plantation. But that's no life for my dearh boy.' A stalk of grey ash fell onto her skirt and she flicked it off. 'They rely on high walls, and an alarm system, and Rottweilers. Anything to

202

deter intruders.' She pursed her lips. 'I tell my dearh boy, it's no life. It breeds viciousness in a man – never able to go anywhere without a gun.'

'Mrs Roberts, how long ago did your son arrange to come over to see you?'

'My dearh, it must be a year ago he promised to come in the Spring. Our Spring, that is.'

'And for how long?'

'For three months.'

'Has he returned?'

'You haven't told me, officer: has he done something naughty?'

'Where is he?'

'The dearh boy's my whole world,' she said dramatically. 'If only I'd created two lovely sons like him, instead of a silly daughter. I loved little boys. Have you a son, dearh?'

'No,' Robeson said, hiding his irritation with a mother who made favourites: 'I'm blessed with a lovely teenage daughter.'

'Of course, not all girls are the same, I know. I had absolutely oodles of sex appeal, and the looks.' She stubbed out her cigarette in a potted geranium on the sill beside her. 'The men used to flock around me. But my daughter . . .' She tut-tutted. 'She's turned out just like her father, a great disappointment.'

Robeson heard the resentment, that she thought she had been let down. In Mrs Roberts's household it had obviously been mother's boy versus displeasing daughter, 'Where is your son?'

'He went up north to see friends.'

'Is he coming back here?'

She passed her hand over her eyes; she looked as if she needed to wear glasses, but was too vain. She fished for another cigarette. 'He said there was nothing for him in this dump. I reminded him, there is his poor old mother.'

'Can I have his address?'

'Why do you ask?' She gave a poor performance of being aggrieved. 'He always was a mischievous little boy. But then, of course, I adored him just the same.'

'I would appreciate it if you'd let me know where he is.'

She looked at Mary. 'The young lady can move better than I can, can't you, dearh? There's a letter on the mantelpiece. It's in there.'

Mary got up. The mantelpiece was chock-a-block with mementos and framed photographs that all appeared to be of Mrs Roberts in her acting heyday. 'Is this it, Ma'am?' Mary asked, extricating something stuck behind a picture.

'That's it, my dearh. You'll find the address in there. He wrote only this morning; you see, he really loves his poor old mother.'

Mary slipped the letter from its envelope, copied the address into her pocketbook, and put the letter back.

'Thank you my dearh, you saved my poor old hip.'

Robeson stood up. 'And I must thank you, too, Mrs Roberts. You have been very helpful.'

They saw themselves out. Their eyes, trained to observe, took in the many photographs of a young Mrs Roberts that adorned the walls; the theatrical memorabilia and clutter that continued into the small hallway with its old-fashioned stand, hung with coats. When they were in the car, and on the way back to base, Robeson asked, 'What did you make of that, Mary?'

'I feel sorry for that daughter. She must be burdened with one hell of an inferiority complex.'

He glanced sideways. 'I meant her mother.'

Mary chuckled: 'Seems a randy old has-been, sir. And she didn't sound really surprised when you asked about the gun.'

'She probably wasn't. But she was an actress, so she says.'

204

'What are your theories, sir, or am I too bold?'

Robeson grinned. Most of his subordinates knew he was about to go in for the kill, when he kept things close to his chest. He said, 'That bullet may have been meant to maim. Or perhaps just to frighten. But . . .' He kept his eyes on the road, the lunchtime traffic was heavy. He filtered into the stream and made for Headquarters.

'But what, sir?'

'What does a single bullet suggest, Mary?'

She shrugged: 'He ran out of ammo, or he ran off, seeing it had found its mark?'

'We'll stick to ran, Mary. Or even perhaps a calm walk away. We don't know which. Yet.'

'He was a good shot. Just one.'

'Not necessarily. Depends what he aimed for. It missed the heart, but ruptured the lung, causing the victim to drown in her own blood.'

Mary made a face. 'So you'll be chasing Mr Roberts?'

'I'm chasing a gun.' He felt her give him a hard look: 'Find the gun, and with the help of ballistics, and forensic, I'll go on from there.'

'But what possible motive, sir?'

He took one hand off the wheel and tapped his head. 'It stays in here until I find that gun.'

'So you'll be going to Derby?'

'Better than a trip to South Africa in its present political climate.'

'What made you ask, sir, if Roberts owns a gun?'

'I know he does. Thanks to research. I didn't need his mother to tell me, only to confirm it and to tell me where he is now.' He slowed down as he neared Headquarters, and turned into the car park. 'And what's more, he has every right to his gun, since he applied to this country over seven months ago for a firearms certificate.'

The jigsaw in Robeson's mind was building up. From his office, he rang Superintendent John Moore, and put forward his theories.

Moore said: 'So you're going up to Derby, Howard?'

'Yes, sir. I'll take Sergeant Mills. I've already got back-up and of course Ballistics will know exactly the gun from which that bullet was fired.'

Moore sounded unconvinced. 'I hope it's not a wild goose chase, that's all. And what motive?'

Robeson had expected opposition. Moore was a bear of a man. A good detective but sometimes only grudgingly cooperative when an idea was not his own.

'What possible motive?' Moore repeated.

'Perhaps only time will tell, sir.' Robeson had some faint notions but for the moment he was going to keep them to himself. He made for the Incident Room, nursing his thoughts. His Division was a good one. Everyone knew everyone, and who the very few problem coppers were; a few liked to leave promptly after their shift to womanise, and one had a yen to live in the pubs, but all in all they were a good team. He looked round for Sergeant Mills: 'Where's Roger?'

A DC looked up from his desk. 'Not back from court yet, sir. He nicked someone last night.'

Robeson swore under his breath. 'I want him as soon as he gets in.'

An hour later, Robeson was planning his tomorrow when the phone buzzed on his desk. He snatched it up, glad to hear it was Mills back from court. 'Get home promptly, Roger. We're catching the midnight train up to Derby. As casual as you like; we're going to pay an early call on a Mr Charles Roberts.'

'A breakthrough, sir?'

'Sort of. We've been hunting a gun round these parts for the past five weeks.'

'D'you mean it's two hundred miles away?'

Robeson allowed himself a satisfied chuckle. 'If I hadn't chanced to stop at St Mark's Church yesterday to kill time, before we knew it our gun might have been back in South Africa.'

Chapter 19

It was daybreak as Robeson and Mills made their casual way towards where Charles Roberts was staying with friends near Derby. The coppers had enlisted the aid of the local nick to find the place, and one of their DCs had taken them to within 100 yards in an unmarked police car.

Robeson confounded the usual image of a Detective Inspector. He was large, admittedly, with a mop of unruly brown hair, but his style was often to punctuate even important missions with a sudden hark back to his interest in ornithology. Now hatless, in an open shirt and a dark jacket, looking more like a modern-day postman on early delivery, he strode several yards ahead of an equally nondescript Sergeant Mills. Stopping in his tracks, the Inspector raised his head to listen. The trees etched against the pale sky seemed to be coming alive; birds were waking up and their first whispering twitters were getting gradually louder and more clamorous in their excitement to greet the new day.

He let Mills catch up and they approached their goal together. It was a two-up, two-down, cob cottage with a thatched roof, and a glass lean-to. In spite of a large chicken run in the garden, waking Rhode Island Reds and white Wyandottes were jumping down from their perches, one by one, and were somehow finding their way out through the wire to strut in jerky, hesitant movements and peck around in the rough vegetable patch outside.

Robeson's heavy knock was eventually answered by a sleepy head from an upstairs window, quickly followed by someone coming downstairs to open the door.

He flashed his card. 'Detective Chief Inspector Robeson, CID. My colleague, Detective Sergeant Mills. Mr Charles Roberts?'

'What's up?' A second man appeared from behind the man who had opened the door. 'I'm Charles Roberts.' He was a medium-size man in his forties, wearing trousers obviously just pulled on. His bronzed chest was bare. 'What d'you want?' he asked, confused and unshaven, his black hair ruffled.

'May we come in?' Without waiting, Robeson lowered his head and stepped from the doorway straight into a living room.

Their police business did not take long; it went more smoothly than Robeson had dared to hope. Roberts was a reasonable man and, once he had recovered from shock and astonishment, with no fuss he produced a gun. It was his own gun; he had had it safely packed since his arrival in this country. He had neither lent it to anyone nor missed it from his possessions. He had expected to have no need of it until he arrived back in Durban where, on his route home, it was not uncommon to be caught up in random incidents of terrifying violence. He had applied well in advance of his visit here for a firearms certificate.

On the train journey home, Robeson closed his eyes. After five searching weeks, the prize was his; the team's; all the boys in blue who had raked through undergrowth, and dragged mucky ponds. But for the moment the gun was his, to bring safely back to hand over to the ballistics and forensic experts for examination.

It was mid-afternoon when the train pulled in. Detective Inspector Mary Starks was waiting outside the station with a car to drive them to Headquarters.

Two hours later, after reports from the science laboratory, and a confab with his chief, Robeson was ready to interrogate Miss Roberts again. He buzzed Mills. '. . . and Roger, if she has no transport, go and fetch her.'

It had been a long day for both of them; a continuation of the night they had spent, unable to sleep properly on the train. But that was Police work; Roger knew it, and so for certain did his young wife by now. Robeson knew that Janet, bless her, had accepted the hard fact years ago.

There were several hours of daylight left. Weeding through his files, Robeson was reflecting on the progress he had made during the past twenty-four hours, when the phone buzzed. He picked it up: 'Robeson, CID.'

'She won't come, sir,' Mills said. 'Least, I spoke to her mother; she said her daughter says she's been here once, so she doesn't think there's any need to come again.'

'Then we'll have to go to her, Roger. Wait for me, and get hold of Inspector Starks, too. She's met the old girl, but we might have to deal with the reactions of two women today; we could need Mary's help, you never know.'

Robeson drove, with Mary beside him and Roger in the back. They drew up at Mrs Roberts's bungalow and went in the gate. But unlike yesterday, there was no redhead with a stick at the window, instructing them to come in. Robeson knocked. There was no reply. He tried the door, but it was locked. He knocked again, this time louder.

'I'm coming, I'm coming,' they heard the old woman call.

They waited. There was a shuffling inside; a series of bolts and locks were slowly being unfastened, and last of all, as the door edged open, Mrs Roberts fumbled to unfasten a safety chain.

Robeson apologised, 'I'm very sorry, Mrs Roberts, I didn't want you to be troubled.'

'She locked it. She did. There's no need till last thing.

She knows I can't manage.' The hooded eyes glanced up: 'Three of you?' She tut-tutted. 'Well you'd better come in if you can get by.'

Using two sticks she moved painfully slowly to the front room. Mary closed the front door and followed the men in as they squeezed themselves between the wall and the hall stand. Mrs Roberts plonked backwards into her high armchair beside the window, obviously relieved to have reached it. Recovering her breath she looked from Mills to Mary. 'Now who is this lovely young man? Is he your boyfriend, dearh?'

Robeson intervened, 'I'm sorry, ma'am, I should have introduced you to my colleague, Sergeant Mills.'

'Now don't start calling me ma'am again, you make me feel old.' She turned from Robeson, and fishing out her cigarettes she offered the packet to Mills.

He had sat on the sofa beside Robeson. 'Thanks very much, but I don't smoke.'

'Well I'm gasping,' she said, withdrawing her bony hand. 'After all that exertion.'

Robeson said, 'I was hoping not to trouble you at all, Mrs Roberts. But I want a word with your daughter, and she wouldn't come to the station.'

'I told her.'

Robeson noted the woman's fresh hotchpotch of skirt, blouse and woolly cardigan. She must be colour blind. He said, 'I want to speak to her.'

'She's in her room, dearh.'

Mary rose from her armchair. 'Can I go and see her?'

'She's in the bathroom, dearh. I heard her go in.'

Mary sat down again.

Looking at her, Mrs Roberts said: 'He's very nice looking, your young sergeant, and so physical. Now if I was a gel again . . .'

She's got a one-track mind, thought Robeson.

She inhaled her cigarette then let out a puff of smoke

that, as it drifted, dimmed her rouged face. 'I always urged my daughter to get a nice man. I never stood in her way like some possessive mothers do, but what thanks do I get?' She shook her head, then tapped her cigarette in the potted geranium on the sill.

Ten minutes of small talk later, which Robeson felt was deliberate and during which he grew increasingly restless, he said, 'Mrs Roberts, you know your daughter better than I do. Does she usually stay so long in the bathroom?'

'She's probably running a bath.'

Mary caught Robeson's eye. She got up.

Mrs Roberts's glance followed her out of the room. 'I was like her when I was a young bit of stuff. The men used to adore me. We had wonderful times dancing the nights away.' She rolled her eyes. 'They used to bring me flowers, and chocolates . . .'

Mary came back. 'Miss Roberts is in the bathroom. I tapped, but she wouldn't answer. I waited, then I tapped again. I think she said "Go away", but she sounded a bit muzzy.'

Robeson did not intend leaving without speaking to her; if he did go, she probably would not be here when he came back – he had met these sort of people before. He said, 'Mrs Roberts, I believe you know the position.'

She was lighting another cigarette.

He went on, 'As much as I didn't want to concern you, if your daughter won't speak to me, I'll have to ask *you* some questions.'

She drew on the cigarette, seemingly unconcerned, as if she enjoyed the company.

He took two polythene bags from his pocket, and held one out. 'Is this your daughter's handkerchief?'

She peered short-sightedly at it through the bag.

He said, 'Can you see her initial embroidered in the corner?'

'Yes dearh, I do believe that's hers.'

'Can't you be absolutely sure?'

She looked closer. 'Yes my dearh, I'm quite sure. She had a box for Christmas. Where did she lose it, dearh?'

Without answering he put it back in his pocket and went out into the hallway. He came back with a rust-red coat over his arm. 'And does this mohair coat belong to her?'

'Yes of course.' She sounded surprised.

He looked grave. 'Mrs Roberts, I must trouble you to go and ask your daughter to come out of the bathroom as soon as possible.'

She stubbed out her cigarette. Slowly she began to haul herself up. Mills went to help her, holding her around the shoulders as she clutched both her sticks. 'Thank you, my dearh.'

Robeson marvelled at her fortitude; she may be an old floozy, but her certain grace and good manners had not deserted her at a time when she must know perfectly well what had happened, and what was coming.

The officers stayed where they were, exchanging glances and filing everything to memory with their police eyes; the clutter of faded programmes, theatre tickets, and showbiz pictures of handsome young men in top hat and tails. On the wall above them hung a large picture of a naked beauty, one breast and pink nipple tantalisingly visible as she peered seductively from behind an ostrich feather fan.

The bathroom was two doors away on the other side of the hallway. They heard the old lady calling through its closed door, 'Hurry up, the officer wishes to speak to you.'

They waited in the front room. Robeson wished he were younger; Roger and Mary looked ready for anything, while his own eyes were beginning to blink with fatigue.

The old lady was knocking hard with her stick on the bathroom door. 'Abigail! Abigail!'

Mills glanced at Robeson.

213

Robeson said: 'I knew that already. Surprising what you learn when you think you're only killing time.'

They waited. Robeson tapped his feet on the patterned carpet. Mills was eyeballing the seductive lady on the wall. Mary examined her nails.

At last, painfully slowly, Mrs Roberts came back. Breathless, she stopped in the doorway. 'She won't answer.'

Mary got up. 'You come and sit down,' she said kindly. 'I'll talk to her.' Standing aside, she made room for the old lady to get by with her sticks.

It was getting dark. The dismal wallpaper in the narrow hallway did not help. The carpet runner was the colour of bitter chocolate, and the wooden floorboards on each side had been stained to match. In the dimness, Mary tapped on the bathroom door. She pleaded gently, 'Miss Roberts, won't you come out and talk to me? Or let me in?'

She waited. From inside came a dull thump. 'Miss Roberts, are you all right?'

There was no reply. Mary tried the door and, finding it locked, she felt for a light switch. Able to see, she tried the door again to make sure, then, glancing down, in almost the same movement she made for the front room and beckoned the men.

Blood was coming from under the bathroom door. 'It's locked, sir.'

'Ambulance, Mary. Then prepare her mother that something's happened.'

About to hurl their shoulders at the door, Robeson restrained Mills: 'No, perhaps better the window.' They raced out through the hall.

From in the garden they soon had the bathroom window open. Robeson helped Mills up first: 'You're smaller than me.'

Mills shone his torch. 'You'll have to come this way too,

sir, she's huddled behind the door.' He climbed over the wash basin that was immediately inside, and jumped down, almost slipping on the sticky wet floor. He pulled on the light cord.

Robeson heaved his great bulk up and into the bathroom with less agility. 'Jesus Christ!' he exploded, getting the picture and grabbing something to make a makeshift tourniquet. He had witnessed such scenes before, but he had not hardened, and his heart beat faster. Blood covered her face, her hands, her legs, her clothes. Blood covered the bottom of the bath, ran down the outside and was splattered over the opposite wall. Blood saturated little mats and had made a sticky trail across the tiled floor to the door where it continued in red hand prints up the door's white paint. It was as if Miss Roberts had changed her mind about what she had done and had been trying to reach the handle.

'Jesus Christ!' Robeson repeated, trying, amid a clutter of knocked-over hairbrushes, cream jars, and scattered razor blades, to save a life from ebbing away.

She was still alive when the ambulance came. He wondered how long a PC would have to stand guard at the hospital ward before she regained consciousness. How long before she would be well enough to be questioned about the murder of Annaliese Meade, or whether Miss Abigail Roberts would not survive her loss of blood; a severed wrist, its seeming admission of guilt.

And so much for mother love, thought Robeson, after Mary had done her usual sensitive best with Mrs Roberts and reported her reaction as more of annoyance than concern or grief. A mother who was probably responsible for her daughter's reputed sexual ineptness. A mother who had only used her daughter's full name to censure.

But his heart lifted. Soon this would be wrapped up. He would be able to give Janet a bit more company. And soon, at last, he would be able to join the Naturalists Group back on the estuary.

It was three days before Robeson got the full picture. He had deduced most, but a visit to Miss Roberts in hospital had filled him in.

At Headquarters, the Incident Room resounded with calls to get out and celebrate with a few jars. 'Congratulations, sir.'

With a satisfied grin, Robeson brushed the chants aside. 'It's been a team effort, you all bloody well know that.'

'How is the woman, sir?'

'She'll never have the use of her hand again, but apart from that . . .'

'How did you get on to her, sir?'

'By chance, Mike. A hanky with an initial A, that growed on a tree. Fibres of a mohair coat.' He grinned, knowing he was baffling them. 'A chance stop at St Mark's Church to kill time, and greeting a vaguely familiar face as if he were an old buddy. I think he was flattered to air his knowledge; he told me about a book in the church, and I learnt that Gail Roberts's full name was Abigail.'

'Was it much trouble to make her cough, sir?'

'There were tears, and recriminations, but she coughed the lot.'

'But sir, how, and why?'

'She had a lift to the church. But she didn't go in. And no one reported seeing an ordinary, local woman in a mohair coat with large patch pockets, walking calmly up Links Road.' Robeson crossed his arms and glanced at the detectives grouped around: 'She went in The Firs by the tradesmen's gate and hid among the trees. To fire her brother's gun, she'd come out and leaned against a pile of sawn-down trunks that were sticky with resin.' He paused.

'Afterwards, she calmly retraced her steps and mingled with the onlookers outside the church before going home and replacing her brother's gun.'

DC Searle blew out his cheeks. 'Phew! I suppose anyone up the road had plenty else to notice, what with wedding people, and the bells pealing.'

'Exactly.'

'But *why*, sir?' Mills insisted.

'Love, Mike. Unrequited, mad, fanatical and desperate passion for her boss, Ian Price.'

'Blimey!'

'She thought she stood a chance, apparently, when he lost his wife. Then she found there was nothing doing – there was Mrs Bray.'

Another DC chipped in. 'Hardly surprising there was nothing doing, I heard Gail Roberts is as subtle as a girlie magazine.'

Robeson added, 'And hardly surprising she went mad. It must have been the end when she discovered she had shot the wrong woman.'

Chapter 20

Helena had blamed herself. If only she had gone with Annaliese for that walk, would Annaliese have been murdered? Would she herself, with acute hearing, have been more aware of a stranger hiding among the trees? Perhaps heard the rustle of movement? Or if she had been anywhere near, would she have heard the click of the garden gate when that madwoman came in with a gun? Why hadn't the gate been kept bolted? Julie was the only person who used it, and she could easily have come in the other way.

Sometimes, when Helena recalled her mother's last words: 'Take care of Annaliese', she tortured herself that soon roses would bloom, but Annaliese would not see them. And later, the trees she loved in Links Road would turn colour and drop their leaves; and in the autumn sunlight they would make a variegated carpet of flame, yellow and bronze. But Annaliese would not see it.

To add to Helena's feelings of guilt, there had followed the shame of Laurence. Exposure of his frauds had not come entirely as a shock. Nor prospects of his inevitable long prison sentence. That kind of hurt was minor compared with her loss of Annaliese.

But in time, an inner voice had penetrated the pain of personal reproach – her friends were right – she had done all she could for Annaliese, and no amount of remorse would bring her back.

Everyone had been so kind. Even Inspector Robeson, with his woman police officer, had been to see her again. Strangely now, knowing everything, she felt less bitter than she had at first. And she was going to pick herself up.

It was an exceptionally warm evening, even for May. In the high blue sky, thin white clouds drifted like tiny whiffs of smoke from a mild cigarette. She drove her car towards the city; the traffic was light. The shops were closed, and the place almost deserted. The pleasant ending to the day had obviously tempted people to get out to the countryside, or down to the coast.

But she was going to a concert. Her first social occasion since losing Annaliese.

Just to have plucked up the courage, and made the decision to get on with life, was doing her good. Or was it the thought that the concert was to raise funds for two charities – Help The Disabled and The Royal Association For Deaf People? And that among the musicians and soloists that she would see, and hear, would be Ian Price?

She took her seat on the end of a row next to the main aisle. Some members of the orchestra were already tuning-up on the stage. The audience was steadily growing, filling the hall with a general buzz and air of expectancy.

She had hardly settled when she felt, rather than saw, someone standing beside her. She looked up.

'How lovely to see you, Helena.'

Her heart quickened. 'And you.' She returned Ian's smile. He looked more handsome than ever in his brocade waistcoat, and a black jacket that fitted so perfectly on his broad shoulders.

He moved forward and rested his hands on the back of the vacant seat in front, so he could face her. 'This is a pleasant surprise. I do hope you will enjoy the evening.'

'I know I will.' She was aware of his sensitive fingers, every well-kept nail.

'Thank you for coming.' His grey eyes held hers. 'Did you come alone . . . in your car?'

She nodded, smiling.

'Oh well . . . perhaps I . . . there's quite a long interval . . . could see you?'

She smiled assent.

'Thank you, Helena. I'll look forward to it.' Smiling, he turned and trod the soft red carpet towards the stage.

She had thought during the past weeks that she had died inside. But as the evening went on, the music stirred her. She wondered if she were an oddity, being a woman for whom the earth moved at the sound of a tenor voice. Not any tenor. But Ian's. It brought a lump to her throat, her eyes stung, her whole body tingled.

She fantasised as the hall filled with his 'M'appari', followed by 'Mattinata', and in Italian, 'O sole mio!' She lived dreams, forgetting that even though Ian appeared to be pouring his soul out to her, in reality he knew that she was still married to Laurence. Until it was otherwise, Ian had shown quite clearly that he was locked in his principles.

She came back to earth. This was life. Now. Today. And Life would go on with its ups and downs, heartache and joys, whatever had happened before. Slowly she smiled inside, telling herself, that time would pass, things would change. And she was an optimist.